"I want to try something," he said, positioning himself in front of her, leaving a foot between them. "An experiment." He dipped his head and kissed her.

Victoria didn't have a lot of experience, but she doubted anyone kissed better than Kyle. Soap bubble kisses, dotting along her lip-line this time. Sweet. Benign. And surprisingly erotic. A scrumptious urge for more undulated inside her.

After way too short a time he pulled back. Her lips followed his retreat, not quite finished with their data-gathering portion of his experiment. She met air. It took a few seconds for her lusty fog to evaporate and her eyes to focus enough to notice his smile.

"My hypothesis was correct," he teased. "We are absolutely compatible…"

Dear Reader

People often ask me how I come up with my characters. Are they based on any one person? Should they fear winding up in one of my books? I laugh and answer, 'You never know.' But the truth is my characters are a conglomeration of traits and habits from lots of different people.

As for Victoria, the heroine in the book you are about to read, I'd say she has a bit of me in her. I am a perfectionist, a hard worker, and I am determined to achieve whatever goals I set for myself. While I didn't have to overcome the obstacles Victoria did, I attended night school to earn my Masters in Health Care Administration while working full time. At the age of twenty-eight I took over as Director of Patient Services for a large licensed home healthcare services agency—a job I absolutely loved.

But with the birth of my second child the measurement of my success changed from a red BMW and a pay-cheque with six figures to being the kind of mom I'd always hoped to be—one who attended school parties and arrived home in time to get my children off the bus. So I left my then dream job and created new opportunities for myself.

I wonder if Victoria would choose the same path? Probably not.

If you're new to my books, I introduced Victoria in my debut Medical™ Romance, WHEN ONE NIGHT ISN'T ENOUGH, the first book in my Madrin Memorial Hospital Series. Roxie's story is up next. I hope you'll take the time to read them all.

I love to hear from readers. Please visit me at www.WendySMarcus.com.

Wishing you all good things.

Wendy S. Marcus

ONCE A
GOOD GIRL…

BY
WENDY S. MARCUS

MILLS
BOON

All the characters in this book have no existence outside
the imagination of the author, and have no relation
whatsoever to anyone bearing the same name or names.
They are not even distantly inspired by any individual
known or unknown to the author, and all the incidents
are pure invention.

First published in Great Britain 2011
by Mills & Boon, an imprint of Harlequin (UK) Limited.
Large Print edition 2012
Harlequin (UK) Limited, Eton House,
18-24 Paradise Road, Richmond, Surrey TW9 1SR

© Wendy S. Marcus 2011

ISBN: 978 0 263 22455 9

Printed and bound in Great Britain
by CPI Antony Rowe, Chippenham, Wiltshire

Wendy S. Marcus is not a lifelong reader. As a child, she never burrowed under her covers with a flashlight and a good book. In senior English, she skimmed the classics, reading the bare minimum required to pass the class. Wendy found her love of reading later in life, in a box of old paperbacks at a school fundraiser where she was introduced to the romance genre in the form of a Harlequin Superromance. Since that first book, she's been a voracious reader of romance, often times staying up way too late to reach the happy ending before letting herself go to sleep.

Wendy lives in the beautiful Hudson Valley region of New York with her husband, two of their three children, and their beloved dog, Buddy. A nurse by trade, Wendy has a master's degree in health care administration. After years of working in the medical profession, she's taken a radical turn to writing hot contemporary romances with strong heroes, feisty heroines, and lots of laughs. Wendy loves hearing from readers. Please visit her blog at www.WendySMarcus.com

Praise For Wendy's Fantastic Debut:

'Readers are bound to feel empathy for both the hero and heroine. Each has a uniquely disastrous past and these complications help to make the moment when Jared and Allison are able to give their hearts to the other all the more touching.'
—*RT Book Reviews* on
When One Night Isn't Enough 4 Stars

**Also available in ebook format
from www.millsandboon.co.uk**

This book is dedicated to Harold Glassberg. A knowledgeable advisor. A staunch supporter. A dear friend. (And the only man gutsy enough to join my mailing list!) For giving me a reason to write and the chance to find out how much I enjoy it.

With special thanks to:

My editor, Flo Nicoll, for your wonderful suggestions and fast turnaround times.

My agent, Michelle Grajkowski, for your fierce negotiating skills and answering my many questions.

My friend, Nas Dean, for helping me with promotion and all things requiring computer savvy.

Some special writing friends, Christine Glover, Joanne Coles, and Lacey Devlin, for your supportive e-mails and blog comments.

And, as always, to my family, for putting up with all the time I spend on the computer and accepting, without complaint, that I didn't cook dinner. Again.

CHAPTER ONE

WITH a few adept keystrokes, 5E Head Nurse Victoria Forley shot next week's schedule off to the nursing office and closed down her computer. Today she would leave on time. She straightened her already neat desk then scanned her tiny utilitarian office to make sure everything was in its place. The memory of her son's tear-filled eyes made her heart ache. "Why am I always the last kid picked up from afterschool program?" Jake had asked last night at dinner. "My teacher gets so mad when you're late."

Mad enough to put Victoria on parental probation. Three more late pick-ups and Jake would be kicked out of the program. Then what would she do?

Victoria hated that the promotion she'd fought so hard for, a bullet-point in her ten-year plan to provide her son a future filled with opportunities rather than financial constraints, significantly

impacted the wide-awake hours they spent together. Although, to be honest, it wasn't actually
the job that was the problem; it was her obses-
sive compulsive need to achieve perfection at it.
To show everyone at Madrin Memorial Hospital
who thought a twenty-five-year-old wasn't expe-
rienced enough to be the hospital's newest head
nurse that she was up to the task.

She grabbed her lab coat from the hanger
hooked to the back of her door and slipped it on.
A final check of her H-shaped unit and she'd be
ready to go. Exiting her office, Victoria inhaled
the familiar, disinfectant fresh odor of pine and
scanned the white walls and floors to assure they
were in pristine condition. She closed the lid on a
laundry hamper and rolled two unused IV pumps
into the clean utility room.

When she crossed over to the hallway of odd-
numbered rooms she saw it, sitting quietly outside room 517. A shedding, allergy-inducing,
pee-whenever-the-urge-hits golden retriever with
a bright red bandana tied around its neck.

So, the elusive Dr. K., oncology rehabilitation
specialist extraordinaire, finally deigned to put
in an appearance on 5E, two hours late for their

scheduled meeting. Well, now *he'd* have to wait for *her* to make herself available. And she was in no hurry to listen to him spout the merits of his program and, she was sure, begin lobbying for her support to make his dog's position permanent.

Not likely.

While she was all for an in-house staff member coordinating a multidisciplinary approach to the rehabilitation of cancer patients and administering daily bedside physical therapy to chemo patients too exhausted or too immunosuppressed to attend PT down in the department, she didn't see why Dr. K. needed a four-legged companion to do it. Victoria walked past the animal, who didn't budge from his position, the slight wag of his tail the only indication he'd noticed her. Okay. So it obviously wasn't a threat to visitors. Still. She was not a fan of unsanitary animals besmirching her unit. Unless it benefited her patients, which was why she'd agreed to hold off on casting her negative vote until after the four-week trial.

"We'll swing by tomorrow morning," a male voice said from inside the room. The rich, deep timbre and his words "swing by" caused a jolt of recognition.

Unease sauntered up her spine. It couldn't be. She looked into the room anyway, had to catch a glimpse to be sure.

A man stood at the foot of bed two. The blinds closed and the lights off, she could just make out was his height: Tall. Shoulders: Full. Arms: Big. Longish, dark hair curled haphazardly over the tops of his ears, reaching the collar of his lab coat in the back. As if he felt her eyes on him, he turned to face her. An unruly swag of bangs hung at an angle, obscuring part of his forehead. Despite his unkempt appearance he was handsome in a rugged, untamed sort of way.

Great. He'd caught her staring.

"Victoria?" the man asked, and started to walk toward her.

That voice. His stride. Please, God. Not him. Victoria felt flash frozen in place. When he emerged from the darkened room into the well-lit hallway, her eyes, the only body part capable of movement, met his. A blue so pale they'd look almost colorless if not for an outer ring of deep ocean blue. Eyes she'd loved and hated in equal measure, familiar eyes in an unfamiliar face, a man's face with a slightly crooked nose, obviously broken at some point, and strong cheek bones. A scar bisected his right eyebrow, another spliced the center of his chin.

But she'd know him anywhere.

Kyle Karlinsky.

Before she could stop it, concern flitted across her mind. What'd happened to him in the nine years he'd been gone? She mentally slapped it back. It didn't matter, couldn't have been worse than what she'd been through because of his irresponsible carelessness. "Victoria?" he asked. "What are you doing here?" He scanned the nametag clipped to the breast pocket of her lab coat. "You're a nurse?" He hesitated, digested his discovery and with narrowed, taunting eyes asked, "What happened? Couldn't hack it at Harvard?"

He'd happened. She resisted the urge to lunge for his throat and squeeze until his lifeless body collapsed to the floor. Instead, she stood tall, well, as tall as a woman of five feet two inches could, threw back her shoulders and lifted her chin. "I'm a head nurse. 5E is my floor."

"You're the 5E bitc—?" He held up both hands. "Sorry."

He didn't look sorry.

She knew what some members of the staff called her. She'd been the victim of name-calling since high school. Snob. Suck-up. It no longer bothered her. "Just because a woman is motivated to succeed and has high expectations for herself and those around her, people feel it necessary to call her demeaning names." She waved it off. "There's nothing I can do about it. But I'll thank you to keep your profanity to yourself while in my presence."

He looked her up and down. "Still dressing for success, I see."

For as long as she could remember, up until the time he'd turned his back on her, her father had impressed, "If you want respect, dress and act like you deserve it." Which was why, when she'd had little money to spare, she'd scoured consignment shops and tag sales to find quality designer pieces to complement the carefully selected clothing she'd been forced to purchase at a discount store.

Victoria took notice of Kyle's black pocket T,

faded blue jeans, and black leather biker boots. "Still dressing for a monster truck rally, I see." Except his clothes were covered by a lab coat. Dr. Kyle Karlinsky's lab coat.

Kyle was Dr. K.? No way! Not possible. Before she'd started tutoring him, she a tenth-grade honor student, him an unmotivated junior, his highest aspiration had been to snag a third-shift job at the frozen pizza manufacturing plant outside town, because the night shift received a $2.00 per hour pay differential.

"You're a few months late for Halloween. What's with the costume?" Victoria asked, trying to control her breathing. While she'd been stuck in the anti-metropolis of Madrin Falls, getting tormented by people more than happy to witness the demise of her seemingly perfect life and raising their child, he'd left town to pursue *her* dream, to steal *her* future.

"Calm down, honey. It's not as big a deal as you're making it out to be" had been the last words he'd spoken to her until today. And they'd been incorrect. To a sheltered, motherless teenager raised to believe sex before marriage was a sin, giving up her virginity to the boy she'd

fallen in love with, the absolute wrong sort of boy who, just a few hours previously her father *had* forbidden her to see, *had* been a big deal.

Life as she'd known it changed that night. And two weeks before his high-school graduation, Kyle Karlinsky had abandoned her to deal with the consequences on her own.

"Not bad." He nodded in approval. "Marginally funny. Delivered with just the right amount of sneer. Looks like someone's developed herself a sense of humor."

"Is that what this is, some kind of prank?" He'd been famous for them back in high school. She glanced at the credentials sewn onto his lab coat beside his name. DPT. Okay, so he wasn't a medical doctor. But still. A doctorate in physical therapy? "No way you made it to PhD." The thought of him staying focused long enough to write a doctoral thesis was ludicrous. "And impersonating a physician is reprehensible."

"Pulling out the big words, huh? Let's see. Reprehensible. R-e-p-r-e-h-e-n-s-i-b-l-e." He spelled it out like he was in a spelling bee. "Reprehensible. Deserving of blame or censure." His smile widened at Victoria's surprise. "Maybe I wasn't as dumb as you thought. Maybe I only pretended so I could…"

Steal her virginity, as so eloquently bellowed by her enraged father.

"I never thought you were dumb, Kyle." An underachiever? Yes. A slacker? Most definitely. Stupid? Absolutely not. "I tutored you. I knew what you were capable of if only you'd have put forth a little effort. But you wouldn't."

"Now that's not entirely true. With the right incentive I was an excellent student." He mocked her, his eyes dark.

"I promise to study for my trigonometry test if you kiss me. Slip me some tongue, I'll get a B." Okay. So it wasn't an approved method of teaching. But, at the time, it'd been the only thing that'd worked.

"I seem to remember," he said, leaning close, invading her personal space. "I did a bit of tutoring myself."

He sure had, with a hand under her skirt in their private study room, up against the cinderblock wall behind the gym, and in a secluded spot down by the lake. At the memory, an unwanted, excited tingle crept out of hiding deep in her core.

She slammed it back, refused to acknowledge it, would not let him get to her. Not again.

"Help," a woman cried out.

Victoria jerked her head in the direction of the panicked voice. A pale, middle-aged woman with dark hair ran into the hallway. "My father. He's choking."

Without hesitation, she ran to help. The morbidly obese patient she recognized as Mr. Schultz sat in an extra-wide chair beside his bed. Mentally she cued the information she'd obtained during morning rounds. Age seventy-two. Status post-CVA six days ago with residual right-sided hemiplegia, speech deficit, and difficulty swallowing.

"Are you able to breathe at all, Mr. Schultz?"

He slapped at his neck with his left hand and strained to inhale, a high-pitched wheezing sound the result.

Quick assessment: Face flushed. Diaphoretic. Eyes pleading. Inefficient air exchange. Victoria pushed his over-the-bed table out of the way, noticing an open bag of colorful hard sucking candies as she did. His daughter was going to get a stern talking to when this was all over. She inserted her hand behind his back and pushed him forward, giving four rapid blows between his shoulder blades.

Nothing.

"Papa. Don't die, Papa," the hysterical woman cried. "You have to save him."

Victoria moved in front of the patient. "Open your mouth, Mr. Schultz."

She could not see the obstruction. "What can I do to help?" Kyle asked.

"I need this bed out of the way." So she could reach the suction apparatus on the wall behind the patient. "Then please accompany Mr. Schultz's daughter and his roommate to the lounge." As stressful as this situation was for her, a trained practitioner, it was worse for a family member/roommate to experience, especially if things didn't turn out well.

"I'm going to help you, Mr. Schultz," she said, surprised at how calm her voice sounded, knowing the man was probably past listening or understanding but needing to say it just in case.

"I don't want to go. I want to stay with him," the daughter yelled.

Kyle spoke to her in soothing yet persuasive tones.

Victoria focused on her task. She reached for the disposable suction container and snapped it into the plastic wall receptacle, thankful her exemplary staff made sure each room was fully stocked with all necessary equipment at all times. Her hands shook. It'd been a while since she'd been in any life-or-death situations. They were not her favorite part of nursing, too many variables outside her control.

"Almost done, Mr. Schultz."

Kyle rushed back into the room. "Should I try the Heimlich?"

"Can you get your arms around him?"

"I think so." Unable to squeeze behind the patient since she was back there setting up suction, Kyle moved the chair like Mr. Schultz was the size of a child rather than the three-hundred-plus-pounder he was.

"I think his belly is too large for your thrusts to be effective," Victoria said. "Position your hands over his sternum instead. Pull straight back. Hard and fast."

Kyle did as instructed with excellent technique but no positive result.

The patient's skin took on a purplish reddish hue. They were running out of time.

Leaving Kyle to continue his attempts on his own, Victoria returned to the suction equipment, hooking the red vacuum tube to the container. She ripped open two sets of tubing, unraveled both. One she connected between the collection container and the wall gauge. The other she attached to the nozzle labeled "Patient", then pulled apart the ends of the wrapper on the curved oral suctioning catheter, and, attaching it to the suction cable, was finally ready to proceed.

"Any luck?" Victoria pulled on a pair of latex gloves and turned back to the patient.

"No. He looks about to pass out."

Yes, he did. If one attempt at suction didn't work she'd call for the code team. Victoria removed the suction catheter from its packaging, turned on the suction device and cranked the knob to high. When she reached for Mr. Schultz's chin, preparing to open his mouth, he grabbed her wrist. Hard.

Kyle intervened, prying the patient's fingers

off her. "She's trying to help you, sir. Let her do her thing."

Victoria placed her finger on the patient's lower jaw to open it. "Open up for me, Mr. Schultz. I'm going to clear your airway." *Please, please, please let this work.*

He allowed her to open his mouth.

Pressing down on his tongue with her thumb, Victoria slid the catheter deep until it tapped something hard that did not feel at all like the walls of the mouth or throat. She pressed her finger over the hole in the neck of the hard plastic catheter to concentrate the suction into the tip, pressed against the hard object very carefully, and gave a little tug. Like a cork had been released, Mr. Schultz sucked in a huge, gasping breath. Then another and another. A coarse but wonderful sound.

Relief made Victoria's legs weak.

Tears streamed from Mr. Schultz's eyes.

Careful to maintain full suction so the obstructing object did not loosen from the tip and fall back into the patient's throat, Victoria eased back on the catheter. A bright red ball of candy stuck to the end.

Victoria blew out a breath.

"You did good," Kyle said.

Mr. Schultz took her hand and held it to his cheek. She patted his shoulder with her other hand. "You're very welcome."

Victoria hit the button for the intercom to contact the unit secretary. "Nora, is Ali back on the floor?"

"She's heading my way right now."

"Tell her Mr. Schultz just choked on a hard candy. He's okay. We're going to get him into bed. She needs to call his physician and come take a set of vitals.

"Would you help me...?" When Victoria turned back to the patient Kyle already had him sitting on the side of the bed. She rushed over to lift his swollen feet and together they pulled him up in bed, although Kyle did most of the work. Then she raised the head of the bed.

"I'm going to talk to your daughter, Mr. Schultz." She put up all four side rails and put the patient's call-bell in his left hand. "Push this button..." she demonstrated "...if you need anything before I get back."

He nodded and gave her a small half-smile

using the facial muscles not affected by his stroke.

"Thank you for your help, Kyle." He followed her to the door.

"Still perfect in everything you do, huh?"

"Hardly."

He took her by the arm. She turned to face him. He leaned in until his mouth grazed her ear. "For the record, my thrusts are always effective. And hard and fast suits me just fine."

Typical. He'd taken her Heimlich instruction and turned it into something sexual. She didn't respond, would not be provoked. She simply looked down at his hand on her arm. He released her and she walked out of the room.

After discussing the prescribed dietary restrictions with Mr. Schultz's daughter and supervising the removal of all the remaining hard candies, Victoria left the patient in her best friend and Mr. Schultz's nurse Ali's capable hands, surprised to see Kyle waiting for her in the hallway.

His eyes seemed softer somehow, not as antagonistic as they'd been. But she refused to let down her guard until she found out why he'd come back to town.

"Nothing better to do with your time?" she asked.

"He okay?" Kyle tossed his chin in the direction of Mr. Schultz's room.

"Much better."

"You?"

"Fine." For a split second she appreciated his concern. Until a suspicion he was up to something pushed its way in. Why was he being so nice all of a sudden?

Nora called down the hallway, "Victoria, if you don't leave in the next five minutes, you'll be late to pick up Jake."

She cringed at the sound of her son's name blurted out in Kyle's presence. The less he knew about Jake the better. She glanced at her watch. "Fudge."

"Still can't say what's really on your mind," Kyle taunted.

"Lucky for you," Victoria replied, then yelled to Nora, "Thanks."

"I'll walk you out," Kyle offered, falling into step beside her, his dog beside him.

"Don't bother." She hurried up the hallway. "I've been walking since I was a child and am perfectly capable of doing it on my own." Apparently that didn't matter. She ducked into her office, grabbed her purse, briefcase, already packed with work she needed to do at home, and coat. Kyle stood propped up against the wall beside her door. She ignored him and headed for the stairs.

"I think I'm allergic to your dog." She pushed out what she hoped were a few convincing coughs. "Would you mind keeping your distance?" Why was he back now, after all these years, when she'd finally regained control of her life? Dread balled in her gut.

She yanked open the heavy metal door, his hand landed a few feet above hers and suddenly the door weighed nothing.

"Since we're going to be working together I think there're a few things we need to work through," he said.

Victoria hurried down the first flight of metal stairs, each pounding step echoing in the empty stairwell. She did not want to work through anything with him, could not get away from him quick enough…or fast enough.

He jogged a few steps behind her.

"To start with," he proceeded despite her silence, "why did you tell that crooked sheriff I raped you?"

Raped her? She stumbled, glanced over her shoulder. "Are you insane? I never..." The words died in her throat as she missed a step. Maybe two. Her right foot hit hard. Her ankle twisted at an awkward angle, her knee buckled. She grabbed for the railing, missed, screamed out as her forward momentum sent her diving toward the fourth-floor landing.

Tori barked in warning.

Kyle lunged forward, caught Victoria by the back of her lab coat and, thank you, God, slowed her fall just enough so he could hook an arm around her waist milliseconds before she face-planted onto cement. Sitting on the bottom step, breathing heavily, part exertion, part fear, she could have been seriously injured. He cradled her on his lap and rested his chin on her silky curls, giving his pulse a chance to slow. As much as she deserved to pay for what she'd done, Kyle had no desire to see her physically hurt.

"You're okay," he said to reassure himself as much as to reassure her.

There were names for men like him, and they weren't ones Victoria would want uttered within her hearing. Why, after that terrifying choking incident and when she was obviously in a rush, did he have to lob the question that'd been dragging down his subconscious for nine long years at her back, where she couldn't see it coming? And within minutes of their meeting up again.

She tried to scoot off his lap.

"Sit for a minute," he said, inhaling the scent of melon, sweet cantaloupe grown in the warm sun, picked from the vine at peak ripeness. She'd always smelled good. Clean. Fresh. Different from the beer-drinking, cigarette-smoking, heavy-perfume-wearing girls he'd been used to.

The feel of her, light and soft, brought back memories of innocent times, holding hands, walks in the woods, the sheer pleasure of having her close, of touching her to confirm she was real and not a dream. Because girls like Victoria didn't fall for guys like him. And yet, in some fluke blip of altered reality, she had.

For a time, Victoria had been the only good

thing in his life. She'd made him believe in hope and possibility, until she'd betrayed him in the worst possible way.

She'd been destined for great things, had been all but formally accepted into Harvard, the alma mater of her father and brother. Pre-med. She'd talked of specializing in neurosurgery or maybe going into research to find cures for cancer, multiple sclerosis, diabetes, and a dozen other medical conditions. With her tenacity, he'd had no doubt, if there were cures to be found, Victoria would have been the one to find them. So what was she doing still in Madrin Falls, working as a nurse?

She tried to wriggle out of his arms again. He tightened his hold, not ready to give her up. And what was that all about? He despised her. But damn if she didn't have him thinking about working off his mad in a few rounds of angry sex.

Because she looked good, better than he remembered. Hotter. Pixie cute, but with class. Her black hair short and perfectly mussed. Minimal makeup. Slender figure. Her fashionable tan slacks and cream-colored blouse covered by an immaculate, wrinkle-free lab coat, high-end shoes on her tiny feet. She liked her fancy clothes, that's for sure.

"You're squeezing me too tight." She started to struggle in earnest. "I don't like being restrained."

He let her go.

She slid off his lap to the other side of the step. "You are a jinx." She fluffed her hair. "Bad things happen to me when you're around." Using the railing to pull herself up, she stood and winced when she attempted to bear weight on her right foot.

He reached out to support her.

"Don't touch me." She swatted his hand away and tried to take a step, quickly relieving the pressure on her right foot. She looked up to the ceiling. "I don't need this right now." Her frustrated yell echoed off the walls.

Kyle thought he may have seen a tear form in the corner of her eye, which sent him flashing back nine years to the last time he'd seen her. Hysterical crying as the sheriff had helped her into the front passenger seat of his patrol car. To spare her the embarrassment of anyone knowing exactly what'd transpired between them, Kyle picked up her panties, used them to clean up the small smear of blood from the loss of her virginity, and stuffed them in his pocket, where the deputy had found them a short time later.

Spending the night in jail had given him plenty of time to think about what they'd done. And she'd come to him willingly with her little moans of pleasure, her desperate pleas for more. Anger worked its way in as he pondered the other possibility that'd plagued him. Had she made the accusation to escape her father's wrath, to save herself from punishment and penance with a total disregard for what may happen to him as a result?

He emerged from his memories, the residual mix of guilt and lingering animosity not quite abated. "You know I didn't force you into doing anything you didn't want to do." So why the hysterics afterwards? It didn't make sense.

"I can't believe we're even having this conversation." She put her hand up to the juncture of her left lateral neck and shoulder, swiveled her head, trying to work out a kink, and locked eyes with him. "I never told anyone you raped me. Look, we had sex. It was my first time. You're huge. I'm not. I panicked. So what? No permanent harm done."

He didn't like the way she turned away when she said, "No permanent harm done."

Aside from the euphoria of experiencing the best sex of his young life with a girl he'd managed to fall in love with, and the rage of having to choose between standing trial and possibly spending years in prison or leaving town for good and never contacting her again, he held little recollection of the specific details of that fateful night. Except for the sublime feel of her, which he'd never managed to duplicate with any other woman.

"Did I hurt you, Tori?" The thought he might have made him sick.

"Don't call me that," she snapped. "Any physical discomfort went away a lot sooner than the pain of you leaving me without a word as to why."

She had no idea what he'd gone through after she'd been taken home? "The sheriff told me you accused me of rape. He dragged me off to jail, let me sit in that stinking cell for hours." While he'd summarized the evidence against him and recounted stories of what prison inmates did to rapists.

To her credit, Victoria looked genuinely surprised.

"It scared the hell out of me."

Her eyes narrowed.

"Well, it did."

"If you'd known me at all," she said. "If you'd loved me as much as you said you did, if you'd trusted me at all, you should have known in your heart I'd never have done such a thing."

But she'd been inconsolable, wouldn't talk to him. She'd pushed him away when he'd tried to hold her and comfort her, fought her way out of the car—just as the sheriff had pulled up beside them. He'd had no idea what was going through her mind.

"At the very least," she added, "I deserved the benefit of the doubt and a phone call to clue me in to what was happening."

"How was I supposed to call you?" Didn't she get it? "I was in jail. And a seventeen-year-old boy with no parents to stand up for him and a twenty-year-old sister too busy partying to care what happened to him didn't get the proverbial one phone call in this town. I was given two choices. Take my chances with a trial or leave town." A kid like him with a bad reputation and no one reputable to stand up for him would never have won a court battle against a family from the upper echelon of Madrin Falls. "I didn't see any way out but to leave. When I was released from custody, a deputy followed me home. I had ten minutes to pack and he escorted me out of town." And followed him another hour after that.

"You haven't been near a phone any time since?" Victoria asked. "Weren't you at all interested in how my father reacted to finding out his only daughter had tumbled, half-dressed, from the back seat of your car when she was supposed to be studying at the library?"

Honestly, as angry as he'd been, he'd still suffered twinges of guilt, wondering. Her uber-strict father was not a nice man. Kyle had thought about calling her. But never had, lowlife loser that he'd been, too busy, working to survive by day, boozing it up and releasing his rage in bar fights at night. Too intent on cultivating his hatred of the establishment, the haves who controlled the have nots, to realize until now that if the sheriff truly believed him guilty there's no way he would have let him leave town. *Idiot*.

"I loved you," she said. "I believed you when you said you loved me."

"I did."

"You did not. Or you would have found a way to get in touch with me to make sure I was okay." The hurt in her eyes coaxed him forward. The familiar urge to soothe her and make her smile kicked in. She held up a hand between them. "Don't. It doesn't matter anymore. I'm over it. So there's nothing more to discuss."

She looked at her watch, inhaled deeply, exhaled, then pulled her cellphone out of her pocket and dialed. Keeping her eyes closed, she pinched the bridge of her nose.

"Hello, it's—" she said into the phone.

A woman yelled back at her.

She held the phone away from her ear. "I know. Strike one. I'm sorry."

More yelling.

"I'll get there as soon as I can." With a press of a button she cut off the irate voice in mid-rant.

"I've got to go," she said to Kyle. Balancing on her left foot, with one hand on the railing, she bent to pick up her purse and briefcase with the other. She looked so sad he actually felt bad for her. "Let me help you," he offered, reaching for her briefcase.

She clutched the strap to her shoulder. "I don't need your help." She mumbled something under her breath that sounded like "Not anymore."

"At least let me examine your ankle. You may need an X-ray."

"I don't."

He watched her limp to the door leading to the fourth floor. "It's unsafe for you to drive."

"Go back to work, Kyle."

"I'm done for the day. How are you going to press on the gas and brake pedals? Let me take you where you need to go." Give him a chance to make amends.

The little color that remained in her cheeks drained out. "No." Her voice cracked. "Really, I'm fine."

They entered the half-full elevator.

Looking straight ahead, Victoria asked, "Shouldn't your dog be wearing a vest or something to make him look...more...?"

"Service dogs wear vests," Kyle explained.

"*She's…*" he reached down to pat Tori's head "…a therapy dog. Therapy dogs are meant to be petted and cuddled. A vest interferes with that."

When the doors opened, Kyle and Tori followed Victoria out. As she hobbled through the lobby, Kyle noticed she didn't acknowledge one person she passed, and no one went out of their way to acknowledge her.

In the parking lot she stopped next to an old black Camry that looked a lot like the one her Aunt Livi had bought a few weeks before he'd left town.

He made one last attempt to convince her not to drive. "So, who's this Jake and why's he so important you'd risk your life to pick him up rather than accept a ride from me?"

CHAPTER TWO

OKAY. That's it.

Victoria tossed her briefcase on the back seat of her car, slammed the door shut and waited to the count of five before turning on Kyle. She spoke slowly, fought to maintain an even tone. "Jake is none of your business. My life is not your concern and I'll thank you, in advance, to stay away from me for the short time you'll be in town."

"Like it or not, most of my patients are on your floor and, once my therapy dog program is approved, I plan to accept the full-time staff position I've been offered." He leaned toward her. Challenging. "The next time I leave town it will be on *my* terms."

"You make it sound like approval for you to bring your dog to work is a given. It's not. We're firm at three for and four against. I'm against." As was her mentor, the director of nursing.

"We have four weeks to change your mind." He patted his dog's head, looking unconcerned.

"No one can be as good as the two of you are touted to be. The patient outcomes and lengths of stay will speak for themselves."

"Oh, we are that good, honey," he said confidently.

"Don't call me..."

"Come on, Tori," he said as he turned to walk away. His dog trailed after him.

She sucked in an affronted breath. "You named your dog after me?" she called out.

He glanced over his shoulder. "She was a stubborn little thing when I started working with her. Reminded me of a girl I used to know."

Victoria resisted the urge to scream. Having Kyle Karlinsky around was going to be an exercise in self-control. And secrecy. At least until she decided whether to inform Jake that his father, who she'd promised to help him search for when he turned sixteen, had returned to town eight years ahead of schedule.

Using the utmost care not to bang her now throbbing foot, Victoria slid onto the cold leather driver's seat.

No doubt Jake would be thrilled to finally meet the man whose picture sat on his night table. He deserved a chance to get to know his dad. At some point. Was now, when he was so young and impressionable, the best time? Until she could learn a bit more about Kyle, where he'd been, why he was back, and maybe gauge his reaction to having a son, she would not risk Jake getting hurt.

Although the drive to school turned out to be a bit more difficult than anticipated, Victoria avoided any major problems. Thank the Lord two pedestrians crossing at Third Street saw her in time to jump out of the way.

The second she got out of the car and set her right foot on the ground for balance, pain exploded in her ankle, the intensity on a par with labor contractions. She eyed the distance from her parking spot to the door of the cafeteria. It may as well have been the length of a football field rather than the twenty or thirty feet it actually was.

Eleven minutes late, she couldn't afford to be any later. Clenching her teeth hard enough to crack a filling, she made a limping dash towards the school. Halfway there Jake exited the building, in the process of pulling on his hat, and without looking at her walked directly to the car.

The afterschool program teacher—Mrs. Smythe—followed.

The temperature dropped a few degrees.

"I had to take care of a choking patient. Then I twisted my ankle rushing to leave," Victoria explained.

"If it wasn't that it would have been something else," the evil woman replied. "I have a life outside my job, you know."

Was it common knowledge that, aside from Jake, Victoria didn't? "I'm sorry."

"Don't be sorry," she said as she, too, walked past Victoria without looking at her. "Be on time."

She would do better, Victoria decided when she climbed into the car, glimpsed into the back seat and saw the unhappy pout on her son's precious face. Jake, the most important thing in her world. "I love you," she said.

He stared out the window.

"I'm sorry I'm late." Victoria started the car and changed the radio to Jake's favorite station.

He lunged over the front seat and turned it off.

Except for the heat blasting from the vents, a tense silence filled the car.

She looked at him in the rearview mirror. "Put on your seat belt."

He didn't.

"Jake, I said I was sorry. You understand why Mommy has to work so hard, don't you?"

Nothing.

It was going to be a long night.

"I'm talking to you, Jake Forley. And we will not leave this parking lot until you answer my question."

"Because it's just the two of us," he said, still looking out the window. "And you need money to pay bills and send me to a good college."

"And so you can play baseball in the spring."

He jerked his head, his eyes went wide. "Really?" He scooted to the front edge of his seat. "You're going to let me play?"

An impromptu, anything-to-cheer-him-up decision she would likely live to regret but, "Yes. And you're going to need baseball pants, a bat and glove, and shoes."

"Cleats, Mom," he said with an eye roll and an

air of eight-year-old disgust at her ignorance of sports lingo. "Baseball players wear cleats."

"After dinner we'll go online and do some re-search." To figure out what cleats were. "Sound good?"

"Sounds great! Thanks, Mom!" He leaned forward and kissed her cheek. "I love you, too."

"I know." But she'd never tire of hearing him say it.

The next morning, her purplish, swollen right ankle elevated on an overturned garbage can and propped up on a pile of folded towels, her neck stiff, and her right knee almost twice its normal size, Victoria felt like she'd been selec-tively beaten by one of the dozens of baseball bats she'd viewed on the Internet the night before. With everything she needed to consider—barrel, taper and grip size, length and weight, as well as material makeup: wood, aluminum, or compos-ite—choosing the correct bat was more compli-cated than calculating a biochemical equation. On the plus side, she now knew baseball cleats were little more than fancy sneakers with molded rubber studs to increase traction on the field.

She smiled. After a difficult start, she and Jake had had a super-terrific—his words, not hers—evening together. He was now an officially registered little-leaguer assigned to a team in the Madrin Falls Baseball League, practices to start next week, the season opener three weeks after that.

It would require creative scheduling, but she'd find a way to squeeze in everything. Work. Jake's school. Her school. Religious school. And now baseball. Her stress level spiked up a notch just thinking about it.

"Knock, knock," a familiar male voice said from her office doorway. "How's the ankle?"

Victoria turned her head in that direction, forgetting her neck felt fine as long as she didn't try to move it. "Go away." She lifted her hand to the stabbing pain and tried to work out the cramp.

Kyle walked in, towered over her, filled her tiny office. He set two cups of coffee on the desk, and squeezed into the small space behind her. His body pressed against her back, pushing her ribs into the desk. She couldn't move. "Wait."

As if his fingers had the ability to shoot potent muscle-relaxer beams deep into her screaming elastic tissues, the spasm lessened with the contact of his big, warm hands on her skin. A pleasant tingle danced along her nerve endings, made her wish he'd branch out a bit. Lower.

Heaven help her, she still loved the feel of his hands on her. Strong. Knowing.

She forced her eyes open. This had to stop. But it felt so good. She let them drift closed, again. One more minute. Maybe two.

But, on the cusp of total relaxation, Victoria's memory kicked in and transported her back in time. Something had her wedged in place. Confined. Squished. She couldn't expand her chest. Couldn't breathe. Could not pull air into her lungs. Please. Not again. She needed to get away. Escape this place. She was an adult, refused to be imprisoned. Never again.

"What's wrong?" Kyle's concerned voice sounded far away. His face appeared in front of hers. Kind. Searching.

She returned to the present standing on both feet, the garbage pail lying on its side. She shifted her weight to relieve the pressure on her right ankle, the move so quick she lost her balance and grabbed on to the desk for support. Her chest constricted, floaters dotted her vision, a wave of dizziness threatened to tip her over.

"You're okay." A strong arm wrapped around her upper arms and basically held her up. "Come on. Breathe. In and out. Move my hand." Which he'd placed over her diaphragm. "That's it."

"I need…" She tried to push away from him.

"You need to sit down for a minute."

Not again. Not now. It'd been nine years, for heaven's sake. Why was his voice, his touch, sending her back in time?

He guided her into her chair. "Here." He handed her one of the cups of coffee he'd brought. "Drink this."

In a daze she lifted a cup to her mouth.

"Careful. It's hot." He removed the lid and blew on it like a parent cooling his child's hot cocoa. Like he would have done for Jake had he been around for the past eight years. Clarity returned.

"I'm fine." She took the cup from him, even though she didn't drink coffee. "Thank you."

He picked up the other cup, took a careful sip and watched her. "What just happened?"

Rather than answer, she countered with a question of her own. "Where's your dog?"

"In with a patient."

"Aren't you supposed to be with her at all times?" Per hospital protocol developed specifically for his and Tori's probationary period.

"Patients open up to Tori. Part of what makes me so good at my job is knowing when I'm in the way."

"Typical man," she said, feeling back to normal, "letting the woman do the work while you go for coffee."

"I brought the coffee up with us. Do you have panic attacks often?"

Not recently. She took a sip of coffee. "It wasn't a panic attack," she lied. "More like an allergic reaction to a new irritant in my life."

He smiled, unperturbed by her verbal jab. "Guess I'd better start carrying around some antihistamines in my pocket."

"I have things to do. Did you come here for a reason?"

"To check your ankle." He squatted down, picked up her right foot in his hand, and slid off her shoe. "Impressive colors. But look at these." He pointed to depressions in her edema. "Your shoe is too tight."

"No, it's not." But, boy, it felt good to have it off.

He gently rotated her foot watching her face as he did. "Decent range of motion. Moderate discomfort. How'd you sleep?"

Woke up every time she'd changed position. "Like a baby."

"Keeping it elevated?"

She pointed to the garbage can. "As much as I can. I'm a nurse, I know how to treat a sprained ankle, Kyle."

"You're sure that's all it is?"

She hoped. "Yes."

A loud bang followed by frantic dog barking echoed through the hallway.

Without a word, Kyle placed her foot on the floor and ran from the office.

Victoria slipped on her shoe and followed.

Kyle slammed into room 514 where he'd left Tori with Mrs. Teeton, a fifty-four-year-old female, ten days post-op radical abdominal hysterectomy for treatment of stage II cervical cancer. Undergoing combination chemotherapy and radiation. Suffering from severe adjustment reaction to her diagnosis, debilitating fatigue, and deconditioning. Completely dependent for all ADLs—activities of daily living.

The balding woman sat with her bare legs on the cold hospital floor, her upper torso, arms, and head draped over Tori's back. "Mrs. Teeton. Are you okay?" he asked, dropping to the floor beside her.

"I'm so weak," she said quietly, her cheeks wet with tears. "Can't even sit up by myself."

Kyle handed her a tissue from the bedside table. "You are going to get through this phase of treatment, and I'm going to show up every day, several times a day, to help."

"What happened?" Victoria asked as she half ran, half hopped into the room, and, ignoring the bits of food spattered on the floor from the overturned meal tray, got right down on her knees next to Kyle. "What hurts, Mrs. Teeton?"

The pale, sickly woman tried to lift her head, couldn't, and set it on Tori's fur. "My pride."

"Before we get you back into bed I want to check you for injury," Kyle said. "Can you move your arms and legs for me?"

"I'm crushing poor Tori," Mrs. Teeton worried.

"A dainty little thing like you?" Kyle asked. "I

think she's mistaken you for a blanket. She looks about ready to fall asleep."

Victoria smiled, a bright, encouraging smile he remembered from the hours she'd spent tutoring him. The one that used to make him feel all warm inside. And you know what? Still did.

"He's right," Victoria said.

Kyle patted the dog's head. "Good girl." She opened a sleepy eye.

With his assistance, Mrs. Teeton moved her arms, legs, and head without a report of physical discomfort. "I'm going to lift you into bed." She felt like a child in his arms. A small woman, like Victoria, Mrs. Teeton had all but stopped eating since her diagnosis three weeks ago, losing an estimated eleven desperately needed pounds. Too weak to participate in her own care and refusing psychological counseling, she had the highest acuity ranking of any patient on Kyle's roster.

Once in bed, Victoria took over, checking the patient's abdominal incision and taking her blood pressure before tucking her into bed. "The incision looks good. Your blood pressure is low. Before I put a call in to your doctor, tell us what happened."

"I'm so tired."

"It's important." Kyle put his hand on her lower leg, touch a big part of his therapy.

"I wanted to give Tori a treat from my breakfast," Mrs. Teeton said, her eyes closed.

"That breakfast is for you to eat, not Tori. And I told you, she's trained not to accept food from patients."

A hint of a smile curved her lips. "Wanted to see. Sat up but so dizzy." She sounded about to drift off to sleep. "Started to roll forward. Tori caught me." She mumbled something ending with, "Good dog."

"That's the most I've heard her say since admission. And I visit her every day," Victoria said quietly, looking at Mrs. Teeton's sleeping form.

"Tori gets them talking."

"Don't sell yourself short." She looked up at him, her beautiful blue eyes soft and warm. "You were great with her. So gentle and kind."

The hint of disbelief he detected bothered him. Before he could call her on it she headed for the door. "I'll call Dr. Starzi. Would you please put up all four bedrails and make sure her call-bell is within reach?"

As he was in the process of raising the last bed rail, someone walked into the room. A nurse, dressed in what he'd recently learned were 5E's trademark lavender scrubs. Brown hair up in a messy knot, girl-next-door pretty. Even with the surprise of her pregnant belly, Kyle recognized her instantly. His friend Ali Forshay, who Victoria had befriended back in tenth grade, as unlikely a pair as he and Victoria had been. Some kids had accused Victoria of slumming, others had called Ali and Kyle her charity projects.

Maybe they had been.

Good, a friendly face. He clicked the railing into place. One of the two he'd hoped to see while back in town. At least he'd thought so until he noticed her scowl.

She observed the patient then pulled the cord to turn off the overhead light. With narrowed eyes and pursed lips she pointed at him and then the window.

Did she expect him to jump?

A second later she grabbed him by the lab coat and pulled him deeper into the room, yanking the curtain partition into place as she did. The second bed lay flat, empty and raised to the highest position with the covers folded down at the foot of the bed, likely waiting for the occupant to return from the OR.

"Why did you come back?" she whispered curtly.

Because Dr. Starzi was the best oncologist around and Kyle refused to pass up the opportunity to work with him simply because of where he had to do it. And what reformed degenerate wouldn't want to ride the success train back into his hometown? Show everyone who'd labeled him worthless and turned a blind eye in his direction except to blame him for things he hadn't done and threaten him away from their daughters that they'd made a mistake in writing him off.

"No hug?" he asked, half teasing. In anticipation of seeing Ali he'd visualized their happy reunion. They'd been pals, both with difficult home lives. They'd looked out for one another. It'd been Ali who'd suggested Victoria tutor him when the thought of failing out of high school hadn't bothered him all that much. He owed her, planned to help her out if she needed it. But from the looks of her, and the size of the diamond engagement ring on her finger, she'd turned out okay, too.

"You're lucky I don't scratch your eyes out after what you did," she said.

And she looked ready to do it. He took a step back, kind of glad to have Tori in the room. "Exactly what did I do?"

"You stay away from Victoria." Again the pointing, this time at his chest. "Better yet, go back to where you came from."

"Hey," he said quietly, cupping her bent elbow. "We were friends. What happened?"

She looked up at him, her expression a mixture of sadness and hurt. "You're not the person I thought you were. I'm sorry I ever encouraged Victoria to give you a chance."

Ali had been one of three people to see something good in him, something of value, at a time when he had been unable to see it himself. Victoria and her Aunt Livi had rounded out the triumvirate.

The intercom in the room sounded. "Recovery Room on line two, Ali."

"Be right there," she responded without taking her eyes off of him. "Do the right thing, Kyle.

Leave. And don't come back. Victoria's worked so hard to put her life back together. She's interested in a man for the first time since you…"

What? Since he what?

"You are the last thing she needs right now."

With that parting shot, Ali, at one time his closest friend, turned and left.

Back in town for two days and Kyle had more questions than answers. If Victoria hadn't cried rape, where had the accusation come from? What was she doing in Madrin Falls, working as a nurse? A caring, competent nurse from what he'd heard and seen, but why hadn't she gone to Harvard to become a physician as planned? Why was Ali warning him off? Why did Victoria's life need putting back together? The most stable, together person he knew, why was she suffering panic attacks? Who was Jake and how serious was their relationship?

Sensitive to turmoil, Tori nuzzled his thigh. He petted her soft head. "We'll find out, girl." And since Victoria and Ali didn't seem eager to enlighten him, after work he'd visit Aunt Livi.

* * *

The small raised ranch-style home looked better than he could ever recall seeing it. Neater. Prettier. The white siding could have passed for new, the once-dingy black shutters gleamed and a bright red door matched what looked like a freshly painted version of the heavy, antique planters he'd lugged out of the garage every spring and back every fall, which sat at either side of the front porch steps.

The gravel driveway he'd shoveled every winter for years looked newly paved, and the grass he'd mowed summer after summer, while sodden from the winter thaw, seemed fuller, healthier.

Odds were Livi had finally snagged herself a man with an interest in home maintenance. Good for her. Only knowing she had a man inside made him feel a bit guilty showing up at dinnertime, with an apple pie and an empty stomach.

The woman knew how to cook, and had never passed up an opportunity to invite Kyle in for a meal. Something he used to thank his lucky stars for, daily.

A boy responded to his knock. That was unexpected. He looked familiar. Probably because he shared Livi's kinky red hair.

"I thought you were the UPS man," he said with disappointment. "Mom," he yelled over his shoulder. "There's a man at the door."

The kid looked up at him, got an odd look on his face. Kyle noticed his eyes, the same eyes that stared back at him every time he looked in the mirror.

"Jake Forley, you know better than to open the door when you don't know who it is," a familiar female voice said from the top of the stairs.

Over the kid's shoulder Kyle caught a glimpse of Victoria, heading toward the door, looking very at home in pink warm-up pants and a white V-neck T.

This was Jake? Kyle shifted so Victoria couldn't see him. "Is that your mom?" Kyle asked quietly.

The boy nodded.

"How old are you?"

"Eight."

Ho-ly hell!

CHAPTER THREE

VICTORIA struggled down the steps to the front door to see who Jake was talking to, stopping short at the sight of Kyle, holding a pie box, his expression a disturbing mix of suspicion and loathing.

"Go downstairs, Jake," she said, needing a few minutes to talk to Kyle, to diffuse his anger before making any formal introductions. Although, based on the way they studied each other, Kyle had a pretty good idea who Jake was. And vice versa.

Her son turned to her, looking hopeful and excited. Of course he'd recognized his father, whose picture he spoke to every night before bed. "But it's…"

"I know. Go downstairs and give us a few minutes to talk."

"I don't—"

"Now." She flashed him the look that said she

meant business then moved her gaze to Kyle. "What are you doing here?"

"Aren't you going to invite me in?" He glared at her, dared her to refuse him.

Every instinct she had screamed: Slam the door in his face, grab your son, and run. She needed time to talk to an attorney to find out Kyle's rights. Her rights. To talk to Jake about his expectations and set limits on the time he'd spend with his dad, if any. To prepare her son for the possibility Kyle might not be in town long and might not be interested in playing an active role in his son's life. And most important, she needed time to figure out how to protect herself, both personally and professionally. He'd almost ruined her life once. She would not give him the chance to do it again.

"No," she answered, hoping he'd leave, sure he wouldn't.

"But, Mom…" Jake whined.

She pointed to the door of his playroom. "Down. Stairs."

"Can I take the dog?" Jake asked.

For the first time she noticed Tori sitting

quietly, looking up at her, watching her life unravel. "No," she said.

At the same time Kyle said, "Yes."

Discord, two minutes into co-parenting.

Victoria tilted her head and shot Kyle her best evil eye, the one guaranteed to make most people squirm. Kyle was not most people. He simply shrugged. "Livi loves animals. I came to see *her*."

"Aunt Livi is dead," Jake said matter-of-factly, and walked downstairs into his playroom. With a flick of the wrist from Kyle, his dog followed.

"Close the door," she said to her son.

Jake did.

Except for pictures and the many stories Victoria had repeated through the years, Jake had little memory of his grandaunt who'd died a few weeks before his third birthday, leaving Victoria alone to care for her son. Not that Aunt Livi had been much help the last year of her life, but she'd tried.

Kyle paled, clutched the storm door, his knuckles white. "When?" The word came out hoarse.

His upset did not surprise her. Kyle and Aunt Livi had had a special bond. *"Despite his up-*

bringing he's a good boy. There's something special inside him. We can't let it go to waste."

She'd sure changed her tune when Victoria wound up pregnant, and Kyle wound up gone.

"Five years ago," she answered. "Heart attack." Victoria still harbored guilt that taking in her pregnant niece against her brother's wishes, dealing with his threats and harassment, and helping a distraught teenager care for her infant son had been too much for Aunt Livi's fragile heart. That Victoria had been at least partially responsible for the death of the woman who'd loved her like a daughter and, in return, she'd loved like a mother.

Tears threatened.

Not a day went by that she didn't think of Aunt Livi.

"And you live here now."

"She left everything to me and Jake." The house and second mortgage. The car and car loan. Unpaid taxes. Credit-card debt.

The news about Aunt Livi seemed to neutralize Kyle's anger, leaving him weary. "May I please come in?" Even though he could have pushed right past her, he stood on the porch and waited for an invitation. "Looks like there's something more we need to discuss after all."

"Now that's where you're wrong," she said, ignoring the cold air chilling her exposed skin, not wanting him inside her home. "We needed to talk eight years and eight months ago, when I learned I was pregnant. Or maybe eight years and six months ago when my father figured it out and issued his ultimatum: 'Get an abortion or get out.'"

"That sanctimonious bastard wanted you to kill our baby?" The usually calm Kyle did a convincing impression of someone ready to do a little killing himself.

"Shhh. Keep your voice down. And watch your language." She glanced downstairs to make sure Jake wasn't eavesdropping. Then she pulled the front door to her back, partially closing it to give them some privacy. "In dad's mind," she said quietly, "it was preferable to people finding out his perfect daughter had succumbed to temptation and gotten herself knocked up by the town's teenage Lothario."

"I wasn't…"

He stopped before he spat out a lie.

"Okay. Maybe before I met you," he relented. "But for the year we were together I didn't touch another woman. I swear on my parents' graves."

"I know." She crossed her arms over her chest and shivered.

"This is ridiculous. You're freezing. Come on, Tori. Let me in."

Come on, Tori. One quick feel. Under your bra this time. I swear I'll be the perfect student for the rest of the hour... Come on, Tori. Live a little. Just strip down and jump in. I promise I won't look... Come on, Tori. I want to show you how much I love you. Let me love you...

She shook her head to clear it. This flip-flopping between past and present had to stop. "The girl you knew as Tori died the day you left town," she said.

"You make it sound like I suddenly decided, hey, let me run out on my girlfriend today. I've got nothing better to do. Why don't I pick up and leave everything I know behind? Oh, and while I'm at it, I can rip out my heart and smash hers to bits in the process." He leaned in, his eyes locked on hers. "If you'd known me at all," he said, "if you'd loved me as much as you said you did, if you'd trusted me at all, you should have known in your heart *I'd* never have done such a thing."

He threw her words back in her face. Maybe he was right. "But you did leave. And since I haven't heard from you for almost nine years, I had absolutely no idea why. You knew where I was. At any time you could have called me to explain why you left, to ask me what I'd said to the sheriff. If you couldn't reach me, you could have asked Aunt Livi or Ali to get me a message. But you chose not to."

Victoria inhaled deeply, tired from a long day at work, drained and ready to be finished with this conversation. "None of this matters anymore."

"It sure as hell does matter." The sound of the storm door banging into the side of the house made her jump. "I've had a son for eight years and no one thought it necessary to tell me?"

"How was I supposed to tell you? I had no idea where you were."

"You were a very resourceful girl who has no doubt grown into a very resourceful woman." His voice turned cold. "If you wanted to find me you could have."

She'd thought about trying, many times. Early

on when she'd been so scared about the pregnancy and childbirth, then again, after Aunt Livi's death, when she'd been desperate for help, for a break from Jake's incessant crying, for protection from the creditors who'd called night and day. But she'd convinced herself if he didn't want her, then she didn't want him. And as much as it pained her to admit it, a part of her had been relieved to not have to deal with the issue of sex between them.

As if during her silence he'd come to some realization, he lifted his hand and ran a gentle finger down the side of her face. "We have a son."

She didn't want his tenderness. Not now. "I know we have a son," she snapped. "I carried him inside my body for nine months. I logged hundreds of miles walking him up and down these hallways when he suffered from colic. I stayed awake night after night because he'd only sleep propped up on my chest and I was scared to fall asleep with him in my bed. I've bathed him, bandaged his scrapes and cuddled him when he's had nightmares. I have taken care of him, loved him, and provided for him as best I could every single day since he was born."

"If I was here I would have—"

"What you would have done doesn't matter. It's what you actually did that matters. And you left. Without a care for me or Jake."

"If I'd known about Jake I never would have left."

"So I didn't matter but a son would have? My father was right about you all along." She took on a husky man-voice and repeated her father's harsh words. "A boy like that will ruin your life, Victoria. He'll find a way to latch onto you and drag you down." She glared at Kyle and asked the question that'd haunted her for years. "Did you even wear a condom that night? Or were you trying to get me pregnant?"

He recoiled like she'd taken a swing at him.

Years of suppressed hurt, anger, and resentment surged to the surface with a force she couldn't contain. "Don't pretend the thought never crossed your mind. My father told me about his visit to the garage to warn you to stay away from me, and his threat that if you didn't he'd see to it that you did. Is it pure coincidence that very evening you surprised me at the library, took me to a secluded spot, and made it impossible for me to say no?"

"This is insane. I never set out to get you pregnant. You're turning a beautiful memory into something tawdry."

"Beautiful memory? You're joking, right? We were crammed into the back seat of your car. I felt crushed beneath you. I couldn't move, could barely breathe."

He looked physically ill. "Why didn't you tell me?"

At first, she hadn't spoken up because he'd aroused her to the point she had to know what came next. She'd loved Kyle, had wanted to be with him, wanted him to find pleasure in her body. But as the car heated and the windows steamed up, as his passion increased and his body covered hers, panic had taken over, transporting her back to that terrifying day in the closet.

Not thinking clearly, she'd allowed her father's words to seep in and take hold. *If you don't keep quiet you'll have to endure it another half-hour.* Keep quiet, she'd instructed herself over and over, just like she'd done all those years before. And using the coping mechanism she'd mastered as a child, she'd imagined she was somewhere else.

After he'd left town, she couldn't help wondering if he'd been able to tell. If he'd found her so inadequate and disappointing that he couldn't bring himself to face her.

"Look. I knew your father meant business," he said. "I thought that night might be the last time we'd be together. I wanted to be your first. I wanted you to always remember it. I wanted you to remember me."

Oh, she remembered him all right, but not in the way he'd intended. "What about what I wanted? Did you give any thought to that? Because I sure didn't want to be pregnant at seventeen. I didn't want to be joked about and ostracized by the kids at school. I didn't want to miss out on my senior year, senior prom and giving my valedictorian speech. I didn't want to forego Harvard to get stuck in this small town, going to community college, and owing years of my life to the hospital that paid my tuition. I didn't want a baby. I didn't want to lose my father's love. I didn't want any of it!"

"You didn't want me?" a small voice said.

Her son's voice.

Victoria stiffened, her carefully constructed world crumbling under her feet. Slowly she turned to see Jake standing at the bottom of the stairs. "Honey, I..."

With hurt, wet eyes and a look of complete devastation and utter betrayal he turned and ran. The door to the garage slammed, followed by the side door leading outside. Victoria took off after him, the pain in her right ankle and knee nothing compared to the lacerated walls of her heart. The guilt and shame of her admission squeezed her chest. How could she have been so heartless, so careless and cruel?

On the third step down, Kyle grabbed her from behind. "Give him a few minutes."

"I can't. He'll run into the woods and get lost. He doesn't have his coat." *He's upset and alone and thinking his mother didn't want him, doesn't love him.*

"You're not wearing any shoes."

"I don't care." She fought against his hold, didn't care if he was bigger or stronger. Her son needed her and nothing would keep her away. "I have to find him. Explain. Oh, God. What have I done? Let go of me." She bit his arm.

"Hell." He yanked one arm away, but held her

firmly around the ribs with the other. "Calm down. Tori's with him."

"He doesn't need a dog, he needs his mother," Victoria screamed.

"What he needs is time to blow off some emotion."

"You've been a father for all of, what, fifteen minutes? You don't know the first thing about being a parent."

"Maybe not," Kyle said calmly. "But I know plenty about being a hurt, angry eight-year-old boy." He turned her, lifted her chin, and forced her to look into his eyes, to see his concern, his caring. "Trust me. Five minutes and I'll go after him."

"I'll go with you. Let me get my—"

"No." Kyle stood firm between her and the coat tree. "I'll bring him back. It's past time he had his father to look out for him."

A father.

At twenty-six years of age, Kyle Karlinsky was father to an eight-year-old boy he'd had no idea existed until today. What the hell did he know about raising a kid? His father was certainly no one to emulate. Didn't matter. He had a son, who was currently trudging through the thick, dank woods behind his home in need of rescue. At least, according to Victoria.

Victoria, who dogged his psyche on a regular basis, his own personal super-ego, despite repeated attempts to purge her with booze and women. Victoria, who'd failed to tell him about his son, denied him the opportunity to know his child from birth, yet had stood up to her father, probably for the first time in her life, to keep their child safe, and had given up her dreams to raise him, virtually on her own.

How was a man supposed to react to all that? Rage wrestled remorse, each one holding their own, while hope and happiness waited on the mat to take on the winner. Which would prevail in the end? He pushed at a tree limb before it scratched his face.

He called out "Tori" again, and followed the dog's responding bark.

Close enough to hear Jake say, "Stop barking. He's going to find us." He smiled. Because that's what dads were supposed to do, look out for their kids, guide them, and bail them out when they got into trouble. If he focused on that, maybe he'd be okay.

On the other side of a wide old oak tree Kyle spotted Jake's red sweatshirt through the scrub, Tori walking beside him. "Your mom wants you to put on your winter jacket," Kyle said.

Jake stopped, turned around. Dirt smudged his damp cheeks, a twig stuck out of the side of his sweatshirt hood, and muck soaked his sneakers.

Kyle walked forward, holding out the jacket.

Jake slipped his arms into the sleeves without saying a word.

"And I'm supposed to tell you there are two juice boxes and two chewy granola bars in one pocket and your hat and gloves in the other. And just in case you need them, I have your boots." He held up the weighted-down plastic grocery bag hanging from his wrist. "She plan on you staying out here all night?"

That got a smile. "She worries."

"Because regardless of what you heard or how she may have felt when she first found out she was pregnant, she loves you."

Jake nodded.

"And that's the only thing that really matters."

A tear formed in the corner of Jake's left eye.

To alleviate his son's upset Kyle asked, "But she has absolutely no idea how tough an eight-year-old boy really is, does she?"

"No, Dad." Jake shook his head. "She doesn't."

Dad. The word hit him with the force of a category-five hurricane. Dad. And just like that Kyle fell in love, wanted to pull his son into his arms and hold him there, wanted to listen while he recounted every second of his life from birth to this very minute. But the last thing he wanted to do was come off like some touchy-feely freak. So he channeled the requisite calm of a cool dad. "You recognized me at the door," Kyle noted.

"I have your picture by my bed."

That surprised Kyle. Even though Victoria would probably rather gut him than invite him to dinner, she'd made him a daily presence in Jake's life and created an atmosphere where Jake readily accepted his sudden appearance.

"Mom promised to help me look for you when I turn sixteen. I didn't want to wait but she said I had to."

As much as it hurt to think if he hadn't come back to town he wouldn't have known about Jake for another eight years, he understood Victoria's thinking. She was cautious, protective of those she loved, had once been protective of him. She wouldn't expose her son to possible disappointment and disillusionment before he was mature enough to handle it. Kyle had been an apathetic teen with no direction, no goals or dreams of success, despite Victoria's repeated attempts to convince him of his potential. If not for the accident and meeting Fig, there's no telling how he would have turned out. "She was right."

Jake looked up in question. Not wanting to address it, Kyle asked, "So what has she told you about me?"

"You like soda, like me." Jake picked a leaf out of Tori's fur. "I have your smile." He tilted his head up to demonstrate and, sure enough, he did. "You're smart like me, you always did all your homework, and broccoli is your favorite vegetable."

He almost laughed out loud. Back in high school he hadn't worked hard enough in school for anyone to think he was even the tiniest bit smart, he'd only done his homework so he could spend time with Victoria, and he ate broccoli, max, twice a year as part of a Chinese chicken and broccoli combo meal.

"So where've you been, Dad? Mom said it must have been someplace important for you not to come visit me."

He'd been turning himself into the type of man a boy would be proud to call his father.

"And why'd you leave without telling Mom?"

Because he'd believed the insults and lies and threats and had been too much of a coward to stay and fight for what he'd wanted.

But how do you explain all that to a little boy? He settled on, "It's complicated." Kyle couldn't withstand the urge to touch his son one minute longer. He reached out and put his hand on Jake's shoulder. "What's most important is I'm here now." He squeezed. "And I won't leave you again."

Jake lunged forward and threw his arms around Kyle's waist, smushed his cheek to Kyle's diaphragm. "I'm glad you're back, Dad."

He returned Jake's hug, wanting to make up for every hugging opportunity he'd missed over the years, yet careful not to squeeze his son so tight he busted a rib.

Tori barked.

Victoria appeared from behind the oak.

"You were supposed to wait at the house," Kyle pointed out. With her foot elevated. He released Jake.

She limped over to her son, and, with a hand on each of his upper arms, held him in place. "Honey, I need you to understand that when Mommy got pregnant I was very young. Daddy left. I was alone and scared. And for a short time I wished I wasn't pregnant. But then I felt your first kick."

"Like I was practicing karate," Jake inserted.

"Yeah." Victoria smiled. "And I couldn't wait to meet my little night-owl baby who made me crave strawberries dipped in dill pickle juice and dry roasted peanuts coated with vanilla yogurt."

"And beef jerky," Jake said proudly.

Victoria made a "blech," sound, and they both laughed.

Kyle's heart ached for all he'd missed, running to the store to satisfy her crazy cravings, watching her grow large with his child, feeling his son's first movements. The memories and private jokes and unconditional love between parent and child.

She moved her palms to Jake's cheeks and bent a bit to put her face directly in front of his. "You have to know from the minute you were born I've loved you with every single cell in my body."

Jake wiped an eye and pushed away his mother's hands. "Don't go getting all mushy." He turned to Tori, who had occupied herself by rolling in some leaves. "Tori's gonna need a bath."

"Yeah," Kyle said.

"Can I help you give her one?" Jake asked.

"That dog is not coming into my house," Victoria answered. "She's filthy." She looked Jake up and down. "And look at your sneakers. I'll never get them clean."

"I'm sorry, Mom."

"I'll buy him a new pair," Kyle offered.

Victoria glared at him. "I can afford to buy my son new sneakers if he needs them."

"But we don't have money to waste," Jake recited, as if he'd heard the words a hundred times before, then turned to Kyle. "Can I go with you to pick them out?"

"Sure," Kyle said.

At the same time Victoria said, "No."

"Mommy and Daddy have some things we need to work out first," Victoria said.

Leave it to Victoria to make the situation more difficult than it needed to be. No matter. He knew how to handle her, how to scratch away at the thick protective layer she showed to the world. What lay beneath was worth even the most exhausting excavation.

"It's starting to get dark," Victoria said. "We'd better head back."

The second time she stopped to rest her ankle Kyle scooped her into his arms. "I don't know why you're being so obstinate. You shouldn't be bearing weight on that ankle. I don't mind carrying you."

She squirmed in his hold. He tightened his arms around her and started to walk.

"Put me down," she insisted.

He didn't.

She started to kick and twist. Her "I mean it," sounded panicked.

He set her on her feet. She stumbled away from him, breathing heavily, her eyes wild, the same as when she'd been desperate to get away from him in her office.

Oblivious to his mother's distress, Jake asked, "Mom. Do you remember when you said you loved Daddy and he loved you and that's why you made me?"

Either Victoria had developed some sudden onset gastrointestinal distress or she seriously regretted her explanation.

She choked out a "Yes."

"Now that he's back, does that mean you're gonna get married?"

The appalled expression on her face would have been comical if the question hadn't been asked so seriously.

Victoria swallowed, wrapped a hand around the back of her neck, and rolled her head from side to side. "No, honey," she said, looking at Kyle. "Mommy and Daddy will never get married. Don't think about it. Don't wish for it. And don't waste your time trying to change my mind. You won't."

Later that night Kyle pondered the events of the day over a few beers at O'Halloran's, one of the three bars in Madrin Falls. The subdued lighting and dark wood suited his mood. A few guys hung around the pool tables. A couple threw darts in the corner. A college basketball game played on the big-screen TV beside the bar. No one bothered him except the bartender, who showed up with a refill each time Kyle emptied his mug.

Unfortunately, his increasing intoxication did not facilitate him finding clarity in his situation. He wasn't looking to get married, so why did Victoria's vehement statement, *Mommy and Daddy will never get married*, bother him so much? Why did she get to decide? What if him being back in town was a chance for them to right the wrongs of the past? What if they were truly meant to be together and divine intervention put them both in the same place at the same time?

He laughed at the sentimental scat polluting his brain.

Damn, he needed a diversion.

As if summoned by wishful thinking, a very female body pressed up behind him and a voice made for phone sex cooed into his left ear. "Hey, baby. I heard you were back in town."

CHAPTER FOUR

VICTORIA did not like elevators, the confined space, the cloying scent of an older woman's perfume, being forced to listen to the babble of two just-out-of-college nurses when she had important things to think about. Like the new transfer from ICU whose arrival on 5E, within the hour, was destined to cause chaos. As much as she didn't like elevators, Victoria abhorred chaos even more. She unzipped her jacket and adjusted the strap of her briefcase over her shoulder.

Second floor.

"I finally met Dr. K. yesterday," the tall blonde nurse, who'd pressed the button for the fourth floor with an inappropriately long red fingernail, said. "In the cafeteria. Your description did not do him justice. He is a major-league hottie."

"And maple syrup sweet," said the brunette with the gorgeous curls, that should be pulled back into at least a ponytail for any hint of a professional appearance. "I'm going to marry that man. Imagine me, a doctor's wife."

He's not a medical doctor, you shallow twit. A little ankle pain and some increased knee discomfort would have been a small price to pay for a peaceful climb up the stairs.

Third floor.

"We all know it's why you went to nursing school," the blonde said.

"If you want to catch a big fish you need to be where they swim."

Big fish indeed.

A third nurse, also blonde but practically and professionally dressed in the green scrubs of the OR, said, "You may want to hold off on ordering your invitations. I heard he got wasted at O'Halloran's last night and went home with Leanne, the secretary in the case management office."

"She's such a tramp," the tall blonde said.

"Why can't she settle in on one man?" the brunette added.

Realization hit. The reason Kyle had returned to town. Leanne. The elevator floor shifted beneath her feet like it'd been jerked to a stop. Only it hadn't.

Fourth floor.

She leaned against the back wall for stability. Pretty, flirty and fun. Leanne, Kyle's on-again off-again girlfriend from eighth to eleventh grade. Leanne, who somehow found out about Victoria's secret relationship with Kyle and never passed up an opportunity to offer her opinion that Victoria wasn't skilled enough or woman enough to fulfill the desires of a guy like Kyle. Turns out she'd been right.

Fifth floor.

On shaky legs, Victoria exited the elevator. The glimpses of a new Kyle, a competent medical professional who showed caring and compassion for his patients, affection and kindness to his son, was a façade. Kyle Karlinsky was the same hound dog he'd been before they'd dated, and she most assuredly would not allow a man like him unsupervised access to her child.

She turned into the 5E corridor and glanced at her watch. Fifteen minutes after eight. At precisely nine a.m. she would place a call to her attorney.

But first, as soon as she walked into her office she called Nora at the nurses' station. "Please have Ali and Roxie come to my office ASAP."

After hanging her coat on the hook behind her door she turned back to her desk to see Kyle, his hair more unruly than usual, his clothes rumpled and his eyes glassy.

"There's something I need to—" he said, looking guilty.

"Shhh. Come here." She motioned for him to move closer. "Bend down," she whispered. He did. She moved her mouth close to his ear and yelled as loud as she could, "Rough night?"

"Jeez." He gripped his temples as if trying to contain the vibration of a gargantuan gong. "Sadist."

"I'm working. Go away." She tried to move past him to get to her desk.

He blocked her path. "I forgot how fast news travels here in Madrin Falls. Victoria, nothing happened."

"That love bite on your neck tells a different story." It shouldn't matter, but it did. Hearing about Kyle and Leanne together was hard enough, but seeing evidence of their tryst made her want to strike out and hurt someone. And since Kyle just happened to be handy… "I don't care what you do or who you do it with. But if *my* job was probationary and *I* was hoping to turn it into a full-time gig, I wouldn't want my proclivity for unsavory woman to overshadow my work."

"Proclivity. Now there's a word you don't hear very often. Here's one for you. Unctuous. It means—"

"I know what it means. And I am not pious or moralistic." Not really.

"Leave it to you to have a working knowledge of a word like unctuous."

"Where'd *you* pick it up?" she asked.

"I read," he said. "A lot. Always have."

News to her. "Well, good for you. Are we done playing vocabulary volleyball? Can I get to work now?"

"Based on how ornery you are this morning, one might think you care about what I do a little more than you let on." He reached for her chin, tilted it up and looked directly into her eyes. "Nothing. Happened. When you're ready to hear the details I'm happy to tell you everything. I've got nothing to hide."

"Except for Leanne's brand. I may have some

concealer in my purse." She studied the offensive discolored blotch on the left side of Kyle's neck, tilted her head, pursed her lips, and tapped her index finger on her cheek, pretending deep consideration. "On second thoughts, flaunt it. It marks you as an easy lay. Maybe you can parlay it into a few more drunken encounters with loose women."

Kyle's response wasn't at all what she'd expected.

He smiled then laughed. "God, I've missed you." And he swooped down and kissed her.

Only their lips touched. His soft and supple, sensual as he pressed them to hers. Familiar. He didn't demand, he offered, exerted the perfect amount of pressure to draw her in. Exquisite. Each one of her protective instincts failed, her thought processes taken over, transported back to innocent times, consumed by rapture. This was what she liked, the promise of more, not the actual more.

"Whooee. If it gets any hotter in here I'm going to start disrobing." The voice of Roxie—her friend and one of the 5E nurses—permeated her lust-clogged senses.

Oh, no. Victoria pulled away.

Kyle gawked down at her, stunned. "I'm sorry. I shouldn't have. I didn't expect..."

"Go," Victoria said. Half in a daze, her lips numb, her heart pounding, she turned away from her staff. How could she have let that happen, at work, in her office? Anyone could have walked in. Her face burned with embarrassment and anger. How dare he put his moves on her, place her in such an awkward position? And why, after everything she'd been through because of him, did she lack the willpower to resist his kiss?

"I told you to wait," Ali said, probably to Roxie. "I told you the dog sitting by the door meant Dr. K. was in here."

"When the boss says ASAP, I give her ASAP."

An arm came around her shoulders. "He's gone. You okay?" Ali asked.

Victoria nodded, but she wasn't. He'd circumvented her defenses. Again. Just like in high school. They were all wrong for each other. She couldn't be the type of woman Kyle needed. And he was the absolute opposite of the type of man she hoped to one day share her life with. Kyle thwarted the rules she followed implicitly. He dissed authority, would never understand or support her need to attain the director of nursing position when the present director retired.

Within five years. When I'm confident my replacement is ready.

Three candidates. All competent. Victoria the favorite. But the tiniest infraction could plummet her to the bottom of that short list in an instant. Something like getting caught kissing a co-worker in her office. And all her hard work to date would be wasted. The opportunity to achieve the top nursing spot, to prove to her critics, her father, and herself that one youthful indiscretion would not deter her from success, would be lost.

Victoria inhaled. Exhaled. Turned to her staff and couldn't contain her smile. Roxie, an extravagant dresser who towered over her by a good ten inches, wore a red, white, and blue polka-dot turtle-neck under her lavender scrub top. At least a dozen colorful cartoon character pins adorned her left chest area. Her rectangular red-framed glasses hung from a bright purple chain at her sternum, the yellow string cord attached to her fuchsia pen and the brightly patterned socks on her six or so inches of exposed ankle, since she had trouble finding pants that were long enough, all combined to make Roxie a walking hodge-podge of color.

Victoria hated to admit it, but if she hadn't worked with Roxie and witnessed her nursing expertise firsthand, she likely would not have hired her to work on 5E.

"Time's a-wasting," Roxie said. "I have a date with a colostomy bag that needs changing. What's up?"

Victoria spoke to Ali first. "You're getting a transfer from ICU. Into room 514 with Mrs. Teeton." Wait for it. "Melanie Madrin."

"Friggin' wonderful."

No need to explain who Melanie Madrin was. The mayor's daughter. State Senator Madrin's wife. And while no one knew much about her, Senator Madrin had a reputation as an elitist, condescending, just plain difficult person. And reports of his demanding and disrespectful behavior at his wife's bedside down in ICU continued to circulate throughout the hospital.

"ICU will call you with a report," Victoria said. "Are you familiar with her accident?"

"Out on Clover Hill. MVA. She was struck

by a drunk driver and sustained multiple, major trauma. Her three-year-old daughter was killed," Ali said.

"Alleged drunk driver," Victoria clarified. "To my knowledge no charges were filed." But that didn't stop half the town from declaring him guilty based on the rantings of Mrs. Madrin's husband. "Regardless, guilt or innocence has no bearing on the care we provide our patients."

"And this involves me how?" Roxie asked, looking at her watch.

"501B. Your patient Mike Graker was the driver of the other car."

"No way," Roxie said, making her already bugged-out eyes even more pronounced.

Mike Graker, the most popular high-school teacher in the Madrin Falls school system, had the other half of their divided town fighting mad about what they saw as heinous, unsubstantiated attacks on his good name.

"How can they put both patients on the same floor? It's crazy," Ali said.

It was a test, Victoria was certain. Would she go running to the director of nursing to complain, allow the publicity and controversy and potential for confrontation to disrupt the smooth operation of her unit? Absolutely not. She would take charge of the situation, handle it proficiently and professionally.

"Each treating physician insisted their patient be admitted to 5E. We're the best." Victoria shrugged. And their superb reputation meant they rarely had an empty bed.

"So what's your plan?" Ali asked, assuming she had one. And, as always, she did.

"Sit," she directed Roxie so she didn't have to strain her sore neck to look up at her. "Please close the door," she instructed Ali while she assumed her position behind her desk.

Ali hesitated. "Are you sure?"

Victoria rarely closed the door to her tiny, windowless office, except when a situation required privacy. "Yes." Then, like a general in a high-stakes strategy meeting, she gave her troops their orders.

Three hours later, a short seventeen minutes after her last tour around her calm unit, Victoria received the call to battle. "Mr. Madrin has Mr. Graker pinned to the wall outside the patient kitchen," Nora whispered frantically through the intercom speaker in Victoria's office. "By the throat. Come quick."

"Come on, girl," Kyle said to Tori as he held open the ground-floor door to the stairwell. He started to climb, took the steps two at a time, welcoming the sting in his thighs, the chance to burn off some pent-up energy.

He'd kissed Victoria. The result, a mudslide of wants and needs he hadn't been able to satisfy with other women. And, boy, had he tried. Victoria look-alikes, polar opposites, dozens of in-betweens who lacked her spunk, determination and sarcastic wit, her innocence, fierce loyalty, and hidden vulnerabilities. In nine long years, no woman had challenged him as much, loved him as deeply, or filled the void inside him as perfectly as Victoria had.

And now, having her within reach, no substitute, not even Leanne, was good enough. Too bad he hadn't realized that before Leanne had leeched onto his neck, leaving what he now knew was referred to as her territorial tattoo.

Not good. Of course Victoria would think he hadn't changed. He had a damn hickey on his neck. And why should it matter what she thought? Why did her jealously fill him with satisfaction? And why the hell was he counting the minutes until he could kiss her again?

He jogged around the second floor landing.

You're not good enough for her, boy. The disgust and hate in Victoria's father's eyes remained vivid in his memory. *You were born to white trash, you live and think like white trash, and that's all you'll ever be. Stick to your own kind, or you'll live to regret it.* Kyle, working at Milt's Garage, dressed in his dirty work jeans, his T-shirt and hands stained with grease. Mr. Forley, impeccably dressed in some high-end designer suit, his shoes shiny like they'd been waxed and buffed that morning. Kyle had never felt more low class, worthless and undeserving.

After the third-floor landing he started to take the stairs three at a time.

Reality check. He wasn't that alone-in-the-world kid without resources anymore. He held a doctorate in physical therapy. And while he couldn't care less what people thought of him, they respected his work. Medical professionals sought him out for consults on patients not responding to therapy. He had a good job, money in the bank, and respectable, high-powered allies in Fig's parents and several of his professors.

He was more confident and secure. No one could run him out of town now. No one could keep him from what he wanted. But what exactly did he want?

By the time he reached the fifth floor, Kyle and Tori were panting. He stopped for a minute, squatted down to catch his breath, pretending to fix the bandana tied around Tori's neck.

The hospital's PA system sounded. "Security to 5E. Stat. Security to 5E. Stat."

With a thought only for Victoria's safety, Kyle made a dash down the empty corridor that connected the bank of elevators with the 5E hallway. He turned. Rage flooded his system at the sight of Victoria, wedged between two huge men, trying to separate them. Good thing the three were located more than halfway down the hall, which gave Kyle some time to reconsider his first inclination, to yank Victoria out of the fray and use his years of bar-fighting expertise to lay both men out for putting her at risk. This was Victoria and she was not the type of woman to appreciate a man's interference, no matter how noble his intentions.

So, hard as it was, he walked to within five feet of her, close enough to dive in if needed, far enough away to let her handle the situation, leaned against the wall, and waited.

"You chose to drive drunk. You should be dead, not my precious angel," the larger of the two men, the one holding the other by his neck, said. "You killed my little girl."

"I'm sorry. Don't…drink alcohol." The smaller man, who was by no means small, just smaller by comparison, struggled to get the words out while fighting against the grip constricting his airway. "I'm diabetic. My blood sugar…low." He broke the stranglehold on his neck. Gasped in a breath. "I didn't know. I wish I could…"

"Well, you can't. My daughter's dead because of you."

"Because of a terrible, horrific accident, Mr. Madrin," Victoria said calmly, and placed her palm on the aggressor's choking hand, easing it away from the neck it was intent on wrapping around. "Please, Mr. Madrin. The police will sort it out. This vigilante justice will only serve to get you into trouble. And your wife needs you. Think of your wife."

Kyle took heart at the relief that flashed across Victoria's face when she noticed him.

The larger man's aggressive stance deflated. "Melanie won't eat, can't stop crying." His head hung down, his shoulders slumped forward. He wiped at his eyes. "She says it's all her fault. But it's not." He lifted his head, glared at the other man, his anger regaining strength. "It's yours."

Tori barked, which she only did to alert him to trouble.

Kyle turned, noticed a thin, pale woman with remnants of bruising on her face, leaning heavily on an IV pole, standing in the doorway of Mrs. Teeton's room. She weaved unsteadily, on the verge of falling. "Warren, stop," she said weakly.

Kyle made it to her side just in time to catch her, and ease her down to the floor.

"Melanie," a man's worried voice called out.

Tori licked the woman's face.

"Get that mutt away from her," a male voice boomed.

Melanie reached a shaky hand up to pet Tori's head.

Ali appeared next to him. "Are you hurt, Mrs. Madrin?"

"No. So tired," she said.

"Dr. Karlinsky," Victoria said, all business. "Would you help Ali get Mrs. Madrin back to bed while her husband and I take a minute to speak in private?"

"Certainly." Kyle actually felt sorry for the man, until he said, "I'm not going anywhere."

Mistake #1: going after one of Victoria's patients. Mistake #2: not obeying a nicely worded direct order. There was no saving the man from the verbal lashing in his immediate future.

"Your physician wants your wife on this floor," Victoria started off diplomatically. "This is where she needs to be. And if you want to be allowed back up here to visit her, I suggest you accompany me to my office." She turned and walked in that direction. "If not, Security just arrived. They can escort you out."

"Is there anything I need to be careful of?" Kyle

asked Ali, turning his attention to the woman on the floor before him, preparing to lift her and carry her back to bed.

"Healing rib fractures, right and left, and a healing chest-tube puncture site on the right. Maybe we'd better help her stand instead."

"I am a state senator, you can't…" Mr. Madrin blustered from behind them.

"Wait," the patient said to Ali.

Kyle, Ali, and Melanie looked up to see what would happen.

Victoria turned to face Mr. Madrin. "In this hospital you are a visitor who is disrupting the operation of my floor, posing a threat to a patient I am responsible for, and upsetting your wife to the point she put herself at risk by climbing out of bed, unsupervised and unassisted, to try to stop you."

Victoria Forley, shoulders back, head high, taking on a New York State senator. A force Mr. Madrin had not anticipated at the onset of his tirade.

Go, Tori! No. This was no girl. She was one impressive woman. Go, Victoria!

They stood at the front counter of the nursing

station in an old-style standoff. Mr. Madrin staring her down. Victoria standing up to him, rigid, unflinching.

"If you don't like your choices, to come with me or go with Security," she clarified, "I'll offer you an option three. I can call the police and have you forcibly removed. Mr. Graker may not want to press charges, but I have no problem giving a statement about what occurred here."

"Please, Warren," Melanie said, her voice little more than a whisper. "Please."

"We need to get you back to bed, Mrs. Madrin," Ali said. Then she whispered, "Victoria can handle him, and I doubt she'll go as far as to call the police as long as he cooperates. Right now we need to focus on you."

Dr. Rafael Starzi was a big man, in every way but stature. Despite his size deficiency he commanded attention, respect and obedience through sheer volume, confidence, and authority, seeming perfectly at ease with his littleness. Kyle liked him.

"Seven days on the job and I have heard nothing but good things about you, Dr. Karlinsky," he said.

"Thank you." Kyle resisted the urge to follow his words with "sir".

"Sit down." Dr. Starzi pushed over a chair. "How tall are you, anyway? Now, I've reviewed your extensive plans of care for each of my patients and am in complete agreement."

Kyle couldn't help feeling a rush of pride. And, well, validation. Dr. Starzi, a renowned oncologist, not only in upstate New York but across the U.S., liked his work. His brusque disposition and businesslike bedside manner aside, people traveled hundreds of miles to be treated by him. A known perfectionist, he was very particular about who cared for his patients, preferring 5E to any other floor in the hospital, and now Kyle to any other physical therapist.

At the sound of Victoria's voice, Dr. Starzi looked to the other side of the nurses' station. Kyle peered around the lazy-Susan-style chart rack in front of him.

"Ah, the woman I plan to marry," Dr. Starzi said loud enough for anyone in a twenty-foot radius to hear.

He'd better be talking about the amazon nurse with the bugged-out eyes standing next to Victoria.

"If I ever decide to marry, you'll be the first candidate on my list," Victoria responded.

Like hell. Victoria was *his* first love, the mother of *his* child, and after the kiss they'd shared, feeling the attraction that still sizzled between them, if and when she decided to marry, there'd better only be one name on her list. Kyle Karlinsky.

The vehemence of that spontaneous thought surprised him because he was far from ready to settle down. He and Victoria barely knew each other. But now that he'd found her, available and unattached, he refused to entertain the possibility of her with any other man.

"Impeccable work habits," Dr. Starzi shared only with Kyle. "Commitment to excellence. Well spoken. Highly regarded by hospital management."

He made her sound like an appealing job applicant.

"And beautiful. Did you know she's being groomed for the director of nursing position?"

No. But the news didn't come as a surprise.

"In four or five years she and I will rule this hospital."

Dr. Starzi strutted out of the nurses' station to stand beside Victoria. Way closer than was acceptable in a purely professional relationship. Kyle's stomach tightened, acid crawled up the back of his throat. Both neatly pressed and stylishly dressed, Starzi topping her by maybe two inches and twenty pounds, they made a nice-looking couple.

"You all set for our lunch date?" Dr. Starzi asked. "We can get a jump on planning our future together."

Victoria didn't look at him, actually blushed.

She's interested in a man for the first time since you...

Victoria and Starzi? Not as long as blood circulated through Kyle's veins and air flowed into his lungs. Sure, they'd make a great Christmas-card photo. But both uber-smart perfectionists driven by a compulsion to advance in their fields, they'd burn each other out. And what would happen to Jake in the process? No. Victoria needed someone to slow her down, to remind her to have fun, to live in the moment rather than constantly planning for the future. Someone to make her laugh, to draw out her warmth and take care of her, even though she was more than capable of taking care of herself.

She needed *him*.

And *he* needed time, to get to know Victoria, to consider the possibility of putting the past behind them and trying again. For Jake. For the chance to be a part of a functional, traditional family like Fig's, like he'd dreamed of since childhood.

But Starzi was out of his league in professional status, pedigree, and personality. The only place Kyle could compete on his level was in bed. No man outperformed him there. Maybe Victoria needed a little reminder of the powerful chemistry between them.

"Something's come up," she said.

Good.

Dr. Starzi moved in close to Victoria's ear. "Next time I won't take no for an answer."

Kyle noticed she didn't shy away. He gripped his pen, envisioned hurling it, javelin style, toward one of Starzi's lust-filled eyes.

Victoria glanced at the oncologist, gave him an uncharacteristic flirty smile. "You always say that." Victoria I-don't-do-public-displays-of-affection Forley was flirting. With another man. While at work.

Kyle located the trashcan, ready to spit to get rid of the terrible taste of jealousy accumulating in his mouth.

"This time I mean it. We're not getting any younger." Dr. Starzi turned to the amazon. "Wha-da you say, Olive Oyl? You got time for some lunch?"

"Sure thing, Tiny Tim. Can you wait five minutes?"

"For you? No. Meet me down at the cafeteria."

"With those itty-bitty legs I guess it's only fair I give you a head start."

"Gigantor."

"Pipsqueak."

"See you in ten." Dr. Starzi turned to leave the floor. "And keep up the good work, Karlinsky," he said. "Glad to have you on board."

Victoria stiffened. Took a step to the left and saw him watching her.

Caught. He forced a pretend smile and waved.

She flashed a look so cold his balls contracted. Then she stormed off.

A few hours later, his rounds on 5E complete, Kyle ventured to Victoria's office. Almost to the door, he heard her talking to someone.

"Hi. Can you stay with Jake tomorrow night from five forty-five to nine-fifteen? My babysitter's sick." Silence. "Shoot. No. Have fun. I'll work something out."

Perfect. He peered into her office. "Is it safe to come in?"

"No."

"I'm free tomorrow night."

"Good for you. I'm sure all the single ladies in Madrin Falls will be thrilled. Shall I send out a mass e-mail?"

He ignored her taunt. "I can watch Jake."

She raised her eyebrows. "Nothing better to do than slink around outside my office? I'll let Dr. Starzi know you don't have enough work to keep you occupied."

"More like I was checking to make sure you weren't holding any sharp objects that could puncture my person."

"Hold on a second." She patted around the top of her desk and looked inside a drawer. "I'm sure I have a pair of scissors around here somewhere."

"Ha ha. What time do you need me?"

"I don't. I'll work it out."

"It's worked out. You need someone to watch Jake. I'm available and I'd like to spend some time with him, get to know him."

He waited for her to say, "That's a great idea."

She didn't.

Instead she said, "I haven't seen or heard from you in nine years. You're back in town for a week and a half. Jake has met you all of twice. You are a virtual stranger, Kyle. There is no way I'm going to leave you alone with my son tomorrow night."

"He's my son, too."

"Genetically speaking." She broke eye contact, gathered some papers and stapled them together.

Ouch. "How am I supposed to change that if you won't let me spend time with him?"

"We invited you to lunch over the weekend."

And it'd been nice. But... "At a crowded diner. How am I going to get to know my son at a diner?"

"I'm not saying you can't spend time with him alone. It's just... I don't know anything about you. Are you married? Living with someone?

Do you have any other children? Addictions? Contagious diseases?"

"No. No. No. No. And, no. Do you want a copy of my pre-employment physical?" he joked.

"I'm serious."

"You know me, Victoria." Better than anyone. "A while back you loved me and trusted me."

"And look how that turned out."

Unwilling to challenge her point, he tried a different tack. "The way you handled Senator Madrin was amazing," he said, meaning it.

She lifted her eyes to his. "Thanks for not rushing in and taking over."

"I knew you had everything under control." He hesitated. "So, I'll swing by at five forty-five tomorrow. I can take Jake for a bite to eat then hang with him until you're done doing whatever it is you need to do." Hold on a minute. Maybe he should have thought this through a little better. Where exactly did she need to be at dinnertime on a Wednesday night? A date with Starzi? Some other doofus?

She smiled.

Damn. Even after all their time apart, she could still read him.

She put her elbow on the desk, rested her chin in her palm and looked up at him all innocent and playful. "You know what? Why don't you plan to come over at five-thirty, just in case I can't find anyone else? That'll give me time to get ready."

Get ready for what? Minx.

He forced a nonchalant expression. "Five-thirty it is."

CHAPTER FIVE

TREPIDATION flitted around Victoria's insides like a passel of hummingbirds, their wings creating a discomfiting, fluttery feeling as she steered her car onto her dark road. She shifted in the driver's seat and gripped the steering wheel with both hands. Bad decision asking Jake if he might like to spend Wednesday evening with his dad. What had she been thinking? And what kind of irresponsible mother gave in to her son's begging and allowed a man she hasn't seen in nine years to babysit?

One out of options.

If not for the presentation that counted for forty percent of her grade, she would have skipped class rather than deal with the angst of the past few hours. And after a busy workday cluttered with the media's attempts to gain information about the alleged altercation between NYS Senator Madrin and the man reportedly responsible for the death of his daughter, she was exhausted. Tack on an accident that closed the highway, lengthening her trip home by forty-five minutes, and Victoria's mind and body were in cahoots to shut down despite her need to remain sharp and in control around Kyle.

She covered her mouth with the backs of her fingertips and gave in to a very unladylike yawn.

Her nerves settled a bit at the sight of his old black pickup truck illuminated by her headlights. He hadn't taken her son and run off, after all. She blew out a relieved breath then took note of her dark house, not one light lit inside or out. Jake wouldn't go to sleep without the hall light on and it was well past his bedtime. She'd gone over Jake's routine, left written instructions. And where was Kyle if not watching television in her family room?

Her bedroom. The only room without a front-facing window.

A snippet of last night's hot, supposed-to-be erotic dream turned nightmare popped into her head. The scent of vanilla candles hovering in the air. Kyle, in her bed, propped up on an elbow, the muted lights from a dozen flickering flames dancing on his naked skin, her mauve sheet inconveniently draped between his thighs. She slammed on her brakes, shook her head. "Go away."

He didn't.

"Come on, Victoria," he'd said in that enticing tone she'd always found hard to refuse. At the same time he'd patted the mattress beside him. "Round two. You're in charge this time."

Dream Kyle didn't balk at the rope that magically appeared and anchored his hands and feet to unfamiliar bedposts. No sense taking chances he'd renege and she'd lose the opportunity to explore and experiment and finally work through her sexual issues and insecurities. On top. In control.

She sauntered toward the bed, swaying her hips. A sexy seductress.

"What's the matter?" he'd asked. "Trying out a thong again?"

Like she'd ever voluntarily repeat that unpleasant experience. Okay. Attempt at seduction, aborted. She'd let the silky, sex kitten robe she'd never seen before slip from her shoulders to the floor, climbed onto the bed and, while up on her knees, scanned his amazing, firm body, careful not to overlook one delectable detail. At least until she reached his massive erection and suffered a visual stutter, could not make her eyes move past it.

"You're going to have to do more than stare if we're going to have any fun at all tonight," he'd said.

So she'd taken him into her palm, gripped him loosely so as not to hurt him, and began a tentative slide up and down.

"Not like that," he'd said impatiently. "You're acting like you've never done this before."

Because she hadn't.

"Come on, honey." He'd tugged at his restraints, sounded frustrated. "When Leanne does it she…"

And so began the litany of sexual comparisons, highlighting all the areas Leanne triumphed and Victoria failed. For someone who prided herself on always being the best, it'd been profoundly humiliating.

Berated and belittled in her own dream. Her first sexual fantasy involving a real man, one with definite convert-to-reality potential, hijacked by insecurity. She'd awoken in a tangle of sheets, mortified and determined to remedy her sexual inexperience once and for all. As soon as she could muster up some lust and trust for a man whose size wouldn't intimidate her should things turn intimate.

Victoria yawned, again.

Too tired to think any more about it, she resumed her drive and pulled her car into the garage. No sense putting off the inevitable. Inside the basement, an eerie light came from Jake's play room—which also faced the back side of the house, she remembered with relief. She walked to the doorway.

The room was dark except for colorful patterns of changing light emitted from the television. Kyle sat cross-legged staring at the screen, some type of controller in his hand, playing a video game, which was odd since Jake wasn't allowed to play video games and she didn't own any. Rage started a slow simmer when she saw two empty bags of potato chips and a flattened box of cookies. In a flash it turned to a hard boil at the sight of her son asleep on the couch along the back wall.

"Why isn't Jake in bed?" she asked, too angry to worry about keeping her voice down.

"Hold on." Kyle jerked the controller and jammed his thumb repeatedly on a button. Something on the screen exploded then he looked up at her. "You're home early. What time is it?"

Actually, she was late. "Ten o'clock." She crossed her arms over her chest. "And I'll ask again. Why isn't Jake in bed?"

"He fell asleep down here."

He said it like it made perfect sense. "When?"

"When he got tired," he answered with a total disregard for the fact it was a school night and on school nights Jake's bedtime was eight-thirty. "It's no big deal. I'll carry him up." Kyle stood and stretched.

"No," Victoria snapped, seizing the opportunity to get rid of him. "Just go. I'll take care of him." She shook Jake's shoulder gently. "Wake up, honey. Time to get into bed." He'd passed the stage where she could safely carry him at age five. She removed the afghan covering him. Her boiling anger surged to pressure-cooker powerful. "He's still in his clothes. Didn't he take a shower?"

"One day without a shower isn't going to kill him."

Maybe not, but it was part of Jake's nightly routine, a routine she'd instructed Kyle in and expected him to follow. "Did he at least do his homework?"

"Yes. That he did. Homework before video games," Kyle said proudly, as if showcasing his good parenting skills.

Hardly.

"Come on." Victoria helped her sleepy son into a sitting position. "Up we go." She leaned in to help him stand.

"I don't feel good," Jake said, approximately ten seconds before he vomited down the front of her. If it were physically possible, steam would have shot from her ears.

"This is what happens when he eats too much junk food," Victoria forced out between clenched teeth, gesturing to the wrappers on the floor. "What were you thinking?" Jake slumped against her, half-asleep, mashing her saturated, stinky blouse into her chest.

"I'm sorry. I wanted us to have a fun time," Kyle said, jamming his hands in the front pockets of his jeans and looking down at the carpet. "Be buddies, our first guys' night." He kicked an empty potato-chips bag. "Junk food and video games are required."

Kyle looked so upset, so filled with remorse she actually felt sorry for him. And strangely enough, she understood. "But he's not your buddy," she said calmly. "He's your son. He needs supervision, guidance and love. He needs responsible parenting and limits."

"You make it look so easy," he said.

"It's not." She smiled. "I've had years of trial and error to get where I am," Victoria said, widening her stance to support Jake's weight. "Don't be so hard on yourself. Give it time. You'll get the hang of it."

"That's easy for you to say. He already loves you. I've missed the first eight years of his life. I owe him so much. I want to make him happy, give him everything."

To get Jake to love him. His sincerity touched a place so deep she hadn't been aware it existed. "Jake already loves you, Kyle. You may not have known about him, but you've been a part of his life for as long as he can remember. You may not have heard him or felt him, but he's spoken to you about his day, kissed your picture and said, 'I love you, daddy,' every night before bed for years."

Kyle's emotion-filled eyes met hers. "Thank you for that." He stepped closer and placed his hand on Jake's head. "I love him, too. And I want, so much, to be a good dad." He moved his hand to Jake's forehead. "Do you think he needs to see a doctor?" Kyle asked, looking worried.

"No. I think he needs to shower and go to bed."

"Let me take him upstairs for you," Kyle offered.

"I'm already a mess," she said. "Come on, honey." She shook Jake gently to wake him and with an arm around his waist guided him out to the hallway. Just outside the door she looked over her shoulder at Kyle. "Please take the video games back to your place and lock the door behind you."

As Victoria walked Jake upstairs, the school's sickness policy ticker-taped across her mind. 'No child shall return to class until a minimum of twenty-four hours after their last bout of vomiting or diarrhea.' Technically Jake's stomachache shouldn't be classified under sickness. It was more gluttony secondary to ineffective parenting. At least, she hoped that's all it was.

Please let Jake feel better in the morning. Too much was happening at work, she needed to be there, absolutely could not miss a day.

An hour later, Jake showered and asleep in his bed, Victoria showered and her clothes soaking in the bathroom sink, she limped to the kitchen to check over Jake's homework and make both their lunches for the next day. Positive thinking yielded positive results. *Jake would feel better in the morning.* She opened the refrigerator door and took out some packages of deli meat. *Jake will go to school.* She grabbed the mayo. *The swelling in her knee and ankle would decrease tomorrow.* She took out four pieces of bread and placed them in the toaster. *The pain would go away.* She lined up their lunchboxes on the counter. *She did not need to see a doctor.*

A floorboard creaked in the family room, the sound unmistakable in the otherwise quiet house. Out of the corner of her eye she saw a shadowed movement. Victoria's chest tightened, her body went cold with fear. Frozen. Until she pictured

Jake cozy in his room and lunged for the knife block.

Aunt Livi's favorite carving knife in one hand, a cleaver in the other, her back to the sink, she looked back and forth between both entrances to her kitchen, wishing she were taller, bigger, stronger. Wishing Kyle were there, not to protect her but to protect Jake if she wasn't successful in fending off her attacker.

But she was alone. Always alone.

Something brushed against the floor plant in the dining room. He was coming from the right. The wall phone caught her eye. 911 on speed dial #1. She dove for the receiver. A man's hand shot out and grabbed her wrist before she reached it. "Stop," a commanding male voice barked.

Like she had any intention of obeying a burglar/rapist/murderer.

She screamed, fought his hold, but he was too strong. The cleaver dropped from her hand. God willing, it would lodge in his foot. When he didn't cry out in pain and loosen his grip, Victoria slashed out with the carver, aiming for his gut. "Cut it out." He clamped his hand around her other wrist and easily took the knife. "It's me. Kyle."

Victoria yanked her hands away from him, clutched her fist to her heaving chest, her erratic, pounding heartbeat palpable through her sternum. "What were you thinking, sneaking up on me like that?" She fought to control her breathing, to keep from dissolving into tears of relief. "I thought you left."

"I stayed to make sure Jake's okay. I feel terrible I screwed up. It won't happen again."

Her mouth so dry she could hardly swallow, she limped to the cabinet by the sink, went up on her toes to reach past the lower shelf that held Jake's plastic cups, up to the next shelf, took out a grown-up glass, and filled it with water.

When she turned back, Kyle seemed entranced by the bottom hem of her nightshirt. She looked down at her legs, bare from the upper thighs to her pink fuzzy slippers. She shifted her stance, felt the brush of cotton on her butt and remembered. Heat crawled up her neck into her face and out of her hair follicles. Of all nights to eschew panties after her shower. Had she just given him an eyeful of her natural assets? From the look of wanting on Kyle's face, yes.

Not good.

"You have the most beautiful legs," he said with a satisfying amount of reverence in his tone.

She wanted to ask, "Nicer than, Leanne's?" but didn't. She refused to enter into a competition she had no chance of winning.

He stepped toward her.

She stepped back and bumped into the counter. "You should go."

"Look at your knee," he said.

Yes. Let's look at her knee. Pale. Swollen. Not at all attractive. A total turn-off.

"Is that from your fall?" he asked.

"Yes. But each day it feels better," she lied. "It's really no big deal."

Kyle must not have agreed because he closed the distance between them, dropped to his knees at her feet, and placed his thumbs where her kneecap should be.

Her nerve endings went I-just-won-the-lottery wild at the feel of his hands on her sensitive skin, until he pressed on a particularly sore spot. "Ow." Party over.

"You might have a meniscal tear. You need an MRI."

Definite downer. Nothing short of total sedation would get her inside one of those airless tubes of horror.

Like he'd tapped into her thoughts he said, "You get the prescription. I'll find you an open unit." He smiled. "I'll even go with you and hold your hand if you're scared."

"I'm not scared."

His touch lightened, turned into more of a caress. He flattened a hand on each of her thighs. "So smooth."

So good, her touch receptors moaned at the feel of someone else's hands on her naked flesh, skilled hands capable of rapturous delight she'd been unable to duplicate on her own. She should push him away and demand that he leave. But a fierce need unfurled inside her, for intimacy and love, acceptance and understanding. And with him kneeling in front of her he didn't seem so big and capable of smothering her.

He slid his hands up further, slowly, sensually. Her body cried out for more. And he responded, continued up, over her hips, and around to her butt. He squeezed, pulled her toward him. "God help me, it's like I never left, like I'm back in high school. I can't stop thinking about you." He pressed his stubbled cheek to her thighs. "The feel of you. Your scent." He turned his head so his nose touched her skin and inhaled. "Fresh and clean with a hint of melon."

Cucumber melon.

She ran her fingers through his thick hair, held him to her, savored the closeness she'd shared with no one but him.

He went up on both knees, moved one foot to the floor and started to stand.

No!

He rose to his full height in front of her.

Back on your knees! Now!

He looked into her eyes with such longing she thought her legs would surely give out, and gently cradled the base of her skull in his large hand. "I have to kiss you." He leaned in and did just that.

It started off tender and sweet. Tender and sweet she liked. Slow was good. But with each passing second his ardor grew. The gentle pressure of his kiss, the tentative introduction of his tongue transformed. Arms tightened around her.

A body towered over her, pressed against her. She couldn't move, couldn't breathe.

Victoria tried to break free. Couldn't. Her visual field narrowed, her chest tightened. Panic. She jerked her head to the side. "Get off of me. Now. I mean it." She gasped for breath. At the same time she fought for her life. Punching. Elbowing. Kneeing.

He jumped back. "Whoa. Calm down." He reached for her.

"Don't touch me." She pointed at him forcefully. "Do. Not. Touch. Me."

He looked at her, dumbfounded. Concerned.

Pitiful. She was absolutely pitiful. And weak. She hated weak. Why did she have to be like this? Tears welled in her eyes. "You should go." Her voice cracked.

"No," Kyle answered, watching her, a trapped animal desperate for escape. From him. Why? "What's going on?"

She shook out her hands in a nervous release of energy, wouldn't look at him. "Just go."

If she kept hyperventilating, she'd pass out

within the next two minutes. "Here." He handed her the glass of water from the counter.

She took it, trembled. Water sloshed over the rim of the glass, splattering on her legs and slippers. Kyle grabbed a dishtowel and went to wipe her off. She reacted like he was coming at her with a knife. "Stay away from me." She held up her hand and backed away. "Go. Just, go. Please." The pleading in her tone was totally unexpected and out of character.

"I'm not leaving until I know what the hell is going on." Why his touch sent her into a panic. She used to love his touch. Welcome it.

She dropped her head into her hand. "I don't want you to see me like this."

Like what? Scared and vulnerable? He wanted to comfort her. But how? Taking her into his arms was definitely out. He settled on, "Let me help you. Tell me what I did to upset you."

From his perspective everything had been moving along splendidly.

"I don't want to talk about this. Not here. Not now." Her "not ever", while unspoken, came across loud and clear.

"Tough."

She squared her shoulders and glared at him. "I want you to leave."

Atta girl. He took a stand, crossed his arms over his chest and leaned toward her. "Make me." That got some of the blood to return to her face.

She tilted her head and quirked her left eyebrow. "You don't think I can?"

Welcome back. "Oh, I know you can. You are the smartest, most resourceful woman I've ever known, and you can do anything you put your mind to doing. I just don't think you will." He studied her. "Because for some reason you're scared of me. And I want to know why."

"I most certainly am not afraid of you." Her words, while haughty, lacked their usual conviction. As if she knew he knew, she avoided eye contact and took a sip of water. At least her hands had stopped shaking and her breathing had slowed. "I'm going to get my bathrobe," she said, walking out of the kitchen. "Feel free to show yourself out."

Yeah, right.

A few minutes later she returned wearing a peach-colored fleece robe over a pair of gray sweatpants.

"I'm claustrophobic," she said matter-of-factly, walking over to the sink and placing her empty glass inside.

"Claustrophobic?" Exactly what did that have to do with anything?

She turned to face him. "I have a severe, irrational, panic-inducing fear of suffocation brought on by tight spaces and feeling restrained."

Restrained? "I never…"

"Maybe you don't intend to. But you're so big." She wrapped her arms around her chest but was unsuccessful in containing the shiver that ran through her. She walked over to the refrigerator and rested her back up against it. "And I'm, well, I'm not."

A horrible thought came to him. "Did I hurt you?"

"No." Her lips formed a tenuous smile. "It's more like a sense of impending doom."

Whoa. "Let me get his straight. My touch gives you a sense of impending doom?"

She nodded.

"Way to grind up my manhood."

She smiled.

"Does this happen with other guys?" As much

as he didn't want to think about Victoria with other men, he had to know.

She developed a sudden interest in one of her cuticles.

"We used to talk about everything." Or so he'd thought. "Speaking of which, how come I didn't know about the claustrophobia?"

"It's not something I talk about." She tightened the sash on her robe. "Dad used to say never reveal a weakness as people will use it against you."

Her father would have made a good general in the armed forces.

"And to prove his point, whenever I was really bad, he used to put me into time out in the storage closet under the stairs." She rubbed her upper arms.

"You? Bad? I thought you were the perfect child."

She smiled but it didn't reach her eyes. "Perfection is in the eye of the beholder. And I'm afraid no matter how hard I tried he managed to find some deficiency or infraction that required punishment."

She stood quietly, staring into the darkened dining room, looking deep in thought.

"I hated that closet. So much junk in there. So dark and stuffy." She shivered. "When I was young I tried to fight him. But he was so much bigger than me. Stronger.'

Hell. Like Kyle.

"He'd simply pick me up or catch me in a bear-hug and squeeze until I stopped squirming." She swallowed and looked down at the floor. "The more I struggled the tighter he held me until I stopped. There was no escape. The end result always the same. A half-hour in the closet. And if I cried or carried on once in there, he'd calmly say through the door, 'If you don't keep quiet you'll have to endure another half-hour.' That shut me right up."

Was that why she hadn't spoken up that night in his car? Because she'd thought she needed to suffer in silence or he'd force her to "endure an-other half-hour"? Kyle felt sick, wanted to bash his head into a cabinet for not realizing, wanted find her father and lock *him* in that damn closet. And, boy, would he enjoy the battle it would no doubt take to shove him in there.

"When I was ten," Victoria went on, "I got punished for something my brother did. I couldn't keep myself from complaining about the unfairness of it. I cried and yelled and threw myself against the door. My dad didn't even acknowledge me. All my thrashing around must have dislodged some of the piles, because no sooner did I sit down, resigned to serve my sentence in quiet, than there was a cave-in. Old coats. Sports equipment. Boxes and bags of who knows what piled on top of me, covered me, pinned me down. I couldn't move, could barely breathe under the weight." She pulled at the collar of her nightshirt and inhaled a deep breath. "But I didn't cry or call out because I knew my dad would only make me stay in there longer. So I cried in silence while I waited for him to release me."

She looked up at him. "Little did I know Dad had fallen asleep in front of the television."

Bastard.

"When he finally unlocked the door I could tell he felt bad, but he didn't apologize. Dad never had to put me back into the closet after that. The threat was all I needed to keep quiet, work hard and follow the rules."

Until she'd met Kyle. He'd had no idea the risk she'd taken when sneaking around with him, felt his gorge churn and rise into the back of his throat at the thought of what she must have been subjected to after the sheriff had brought her home, at the mercy of her sadistic father.

She shook her head as if trying to clear the past and return to the present. "Anyway," she said, "that night in your car it was so stuffy and cramped. You were so heavy on top of me. I felt trapped. Squashed. It took me back to the closet." She palmed the back of her neck and stretched it out. "And now every time you touch me I feel on the brink of returning there and I panic. I don't want to revisit that place. I can't stand what it does to me."

While he'd been experiencing a sexual epiphany, she'd been gasping for breath beneath him, reliving a horrible experience. And he'd been oblivious. God help him. He deserved to have an ice pick shoved into his eye. "You should have told me." He would have done things differently, made it easier for her.

"It's getting late." She pushed off the refrigerator. "I need to get some sleep."

"You never answered my question. Do you get this panicky sense of impending doom with other men, or just me?"

Instead of answering, she walked over to the toaster and started to make sandwiches.

He waited, watched her economy of movements, like she performed the same motions night after night, week after week, month after month. Ever efficient.

After putting both lunchboxes in the refrigerator and wiping down the counter, she threw the sponge into the sink and blurted, "You're going to make me say it, aren't you?"

He leaned against a cabinet, crossed one foot over the other, prepared to wait as long as it took.

"Fine. There haven't been any other men."

That pleased him way more than it should have.

She flung her arms into the air. "Exactly when was I supposed to snag myself another boyfriend? When I was seventeen and heartbroken and pregnant? When I was taking care of an infant and trying to graduate high school? When I was eighteen, nineteen, or twenty, taking care of a baby and a sick aunt while working and going to college? Or any time after that while I was raising an impressionable young son, on my own, working to create a better life for us, struggling to pay off Aunt Livi's creditors, to keep my house, and maintain my sanity? Who on earth do you think would have wanted me?"

He would have. In the tick of a clock, the beat of a song, without one millisecond of hesitation.

"No one worthwhile," she snapped.

Or was that all just a huge rationalization for the real problem? She was scared.

"I needed to make something of myself. I needed to turn my life into something I'm proud to share with someone else."

"And now that you have, you want Dr. Starzi?"

"Don't say his name like that. We're the same type of people. We want the same things."

"Then answer me this," Kyle said. "If you like him so much, why didn't you tell me to stop when I kissed you in your office? Why did you kiss me back like you'd dreamed about it for years, like you needed it to sustain your very life?" She hadn't panicked then.

"Who knew you had such a flair for the dramatic?" she said. "You should try your hand at writing romance."

"You read a lot of romance books? Do you get all hot and achy with want when the hero uses his tongue to make the heroine—?"

"Stop it."

Gotcha. He walked toward her. She didn't back away. Good. She stood with her hands balled into fists at her sides. Defiant.

He lifted a finger to tuck a soft curl behind her ear. "I'm not a randy seventeen-year-old kid anymore. I know how to take care of a woman, how to give her what she craves."

Victoria swallowed. "Well, good for you, because despite the rumored praise from your many high-school paramours, from my recollection, there was a lot of room for improvement."

And with that *whack* from her verbal mallet, the ground bits of his manhood were flattened into unrecognizable form. He'd disappointed the one girl who'd mattered, the one he'd wanted most to please. "Maybe you should give me an opportunity for a re-do," he suggested, wanting it more than just about anything. He leaned in close, careful not to touch her. "Let me show you how good it can be, how amazing I can make you feel."

She stared up at him, knowing Victoria, running every possible option with each responding outcome through her head. After what seemed like an hour she said, "I'd have to be on top."

Limiting, but doable. "Anything you want."

"What if I insisted on tying you to my bed and gagging you?"

A dominatrix? Not Victoria. Bossy, yes. A control freak. Most definitely. But into sexual bondage and domination? Absolutely not. There was something more going on. He called her bluff. "I'm always open to new experiences."

"Good." She surprised him. "I have some rope in the garage."

CHAPTER SIX

"THEN what?" Ali asked with eager anticipation after Victoria finished explaining the details of her previous night's encounter with Kyle.

"I went down to look for the rope." Which she'd found instantly thanks to being compulsively organized. Then she'd spent a good fifteen minutes pacing, trying to work up the courage to go back upstairs. Her problems had started with him, so he should be the one to help her work through them, right? "Is it hot in here?" Victoria picked up a manila folder from her desk and used it as a fan.

"You can open the door as soon as you tell me what happened next." Ali shifted to the edge of her seat.

"Oh, yes. How can I not share the best part? On my way upstairs…" Nervous about what she'd decided to do, excited to finally have the chance to test out her theory: She'd be fine with sex as long as she could be on top and in control. "I met Kyle heading downstairs. He said it'd occurred to him he didn't have any protection and unless I had some condoms around, which I'm sure he knew I didn't, he'd have to take a rain check."

"Didn't have any protection?"

"I know. Lame, with a capital L." Men like Kyle always had protection stashed somewhere on their person. She'd almost asked to see his wallet so she could check for herself, the sure sign of a desperate woman.

So what if he flirted and teased, that's what Kyle did. Give him some time to really consider her lack of experience coupled with her psychotic aversion to suffocation and he wanted no part of her, ran like her afflictions were contagious and further exposure would render him impotent.

"I'm sorry," Ali said.

Unable to tolerate the confines of her cell-like office for one more minute, Victoria stood and whipped open the door, to see Kyle.

"You're an idiot," Ali said to him as she squeezed past to exit the office.

"Ouch." Kyle flattened his palm over right nipple. "Don't you think it's about time you give up that annoying pinching habit?" he called after her.

With Kyle occupied, Victoria tried to slip out behind Ali. No such luck.

He stepped to the side, blocking her path to freedom. "No sense asking what you two ladies were talking about. Still no secrets between you?"

"Very few."

He leaned against the doorframe all relaxed and casual and in her way. "I came to see if you'd have lunch with me."

After last night? Not even if she were starving and he held the last sandwich within a hundred-mile radius. "I brought my lunch, sorry."

"What about dinner? You, me and Jake. You choose the restaurant. My treat."

A peace offering. Not interested. "Busy."

"How about Friday?"

"We already have plans." Not.

"I'd like to take Jake shopping for a baseball glove," he said.

Not happening. Victoria would be buying her son his first glove. "And what exactly do you know about baseball gloves?" He didn't play baseball. Did he think shopping for sports equipment required a set of testicles?

"They need to feel comfortable and catch baseballs."

A typical Kyle answer. "Can you tell the difference between a glove meant for baseball and one for softball? What about infielder and outfielder gloves? Leftie, righty, and catchers' gloves?"

"I'm guessing I can figure it out."

"Did you know glove size varies according to what position a child plays? That there's a certain measurement you need to…"

He held up a hand to stop her dissertation. "We'll all go. Bind up your research and bring it along. How about Saturday?"

"Busy." Taking her son shopping for his new baseball glove, followed by lunch at the mall, just the two of them.

Kyle narrowed his eyes, finally catching onto the trend. "So what day *is* Jake free?"

"Why don't you give me your attorney's name and he and my attorney can work out a visitation schedule?" Time to create some distance between them, to let him know he couldn't swing back into town on a whim and mess with her life.

"I get it." He crossed his arms over his chest. "You're mad. I changed my mind and decided I didn't want to be your trussed-up sex toy with a pulse. Sorry I disappointed you."

Of all the unprofessional, inappropriate, truly awful things to say. Victoria grabbed Kyle by the T-shirt, yanked him into her office, and after sticking her head out into the hallway to make sure no one overheard his crass remark, shut the door behind her. "Don't you ever talk to me like that at work." He made it sound so hideous and objectionable. She'd had every intention of satisfying him, or at least giving it her best attempt, multiple attempts if necessary.

"So at home it's okay?" He glared down at her.

He had no reason to be mad. She was the one who'd been rejected. "It's rude and base and never okay. What's the matter with you?"

"Maybe I'm a little pissed myself. Maybe I'm insulted that the only way you'll have me in your bed is tied down, like I present some sort of threat, like you don't trust I'll be careful with you."

So he'd figured her out. Give that man his pick from the wall of prizes. "Actually, I'm a wicked person, a staunch sexual deviant. And if being trussed up isn't something you're comfortable with..." she shook her head "...I'm afraid we're not at all compatible."

"Cut it out, Victoria."

Fine. "It was not my intention to insult you." She made it a point to look him in the eyes. "For that, I'm sorry." On most days, Victoria couldn't sit in her office for more than five minutes without someone needing something. Now, when she could really use an interruption, no one bothered her.

"I want to try something," he said, positioning himself in front of her, leaving a foot between them. "An experiment." He dipped his head and kissed her.

Victoria didn't have a lot of experience, but she doubted anyone kissed better than Kyle. Soap-bubble kisses, dotting along her lip line this time. Sweet. Benign. And surprisingly erotic. A scrumptious urge for more undulated inside her.

After way too short a time, he pulled back. Her lips followed his retreat, not quite finished with the data-gathering portion of his experiment. She met air. It took a few seconds for her lusty fog to evaporate and her eyes to focus enough to notice his smile.

"My hypothesis was correct," he teased. "We are absolutely compatible. You still like my kisses." He lifted his hand slowly and eased it behind her neck, slid his long fingers up the base of her scalp, into her hair. Before she could stop them, her head dropped back into his palm, and her lungs released a relaxing breath.

"You still like my touch," he said.

Oh, yeah. But innocent kissing and touching weren't the problem.

"And you want my body." He lifted her hand and placed it on his firm chest, the definition of his muscles evident through the soft cotton T. "Even if you only want it tied to your bed," he half joked.

"It was a silly idea, from a dream. I shouldn't have..."

"What did you do to me while you had me under your control in this dream of yours?"

"Nothing." She shoved him away.

At his look of surprise she explained, "You would not stop talking."

"Which explains the gag. Okay. Limit the

verbal nasties while in bed with Victoria," he said with an air check. "Got it."

"You weren't talking dirty, you idiot. You wouldn't stop comparing me to…" Uh-oh. Too much information. "Don't you have someplace you need to be? Or is Tori doing all your work again?"

"Comparing you?"

"It's silly. No big deal. Just a dream."

"Who did I compare you to?"

Man, he could sure focus when he wanted to. "Leanne. Okay? It never took Leanne so long to blah, blah, blah," Victoria mimicked dream Kyle. "When Leanne does it she blah, blah, blah."

Real Kyle smiled.

"It's not funny. Leanne is perfect. Tall. Pretty. Voluptuous." Victoria was the antonym of voluptuous. "And she's good at sex while I'm…" Not. Might as well put it out there.

"She's also vain, manipulative, and self-centered," Kyle countered. "And to clarify, nothing happened between Leanne and me. She drove me home, tried to renew our *friendship*. But when I closed my eyes it was your face I saw. It was you I wanted kissing me, your hands I wanted touching me."

Victoria tried to stifle the thrill of hearing he wanted her more than Leanne.

"So I got out of there," Kyle continued. "But from what I remember and the rumors I've heard around the hospital, Leanne is not just good at sex, she's great at sex."

Thrill effectively stifled. "Thank you for all that unwanted information."

"Do you want to know what makes Leanne so great at sex?"

"Not really. No."

He told her anyway. "She does it with a lot of guys."

"Good to know," Victoria said, unable to look at him. "I'll get right on it."

"She practices." His voice dropped an octave and he reached out to turn her chin in his direction. He leaned in, putting his handsome face directly in front of hers. "And you can get right on it, with me. Any time. Anywhere."

Of course someone would choose that exact moment to knock.

"Think about it," Kyle whispered in her ear.

"You don't have to tie me down to have your way with me."

How did one respond to an offer of that nature, while at work, with someone waiting, possibly listening, on the other side of the door?

"It will be so much better than those trashy books you read," he said seductively, his hot breath on her ear sending an ill-timed flush of arousing warmth through her.

So he *had* snooped in her bedroom. "I live vicariously."

"Not anymore." His words held equal parts of confidence and promise.

Victoria wished she'd replaced her oscillating fan when the motor had burned out.

Another knock, more insistent this time.

Kyle opened the door.

The director of nursing stood in the hallway.

Of all people, why her? Why now?

The dark gray suit she wore matched her hair and was flatteringly fitted on her rotund shape. A tallish woman, the sensible pumps she wore, an outdated style Victoria would never be caught dead in, brought her forehead level with Kyle's nose. She shifted her eyes from Victoria to Kyle then back to Victoria. Knowing. Disapproving.

Not good. Victoria felt like a child about to be reprimanded, caught in a compromising situation by the woman who controlled her future.

"Thank you for your time," Kyle said to Victoria, using his professional voice. "If you have any further questions don't hesitate to ask. And I'll wait to hear back from you about the matter we discussed."

If she flicked water on her face it would surely sizzle.

"Where is your *pet*, Dr. Karlinsky?" The director asked, doing an impressive job of looking down her nose at Kyle, who stood a good six inches taller.

"If you're referring to my *therapy dog*, Tori, a patient requested a few minutes alone with her. And I'd best be getting back to them." The director watched Kyle walk away then shifted a condemning gaze to Victoria. "Don't ruin everything you've worked so hard to achieve by getting involved with a man like that," she warned, and entered Victoria's office, closing the door behind her.

One of the highly anticipated perks of becoming director of nursing was that Victoria would have a window in her office, allowing immediate access to fresh, breathable air whenever the need arose. What she wouldn't give for the ability to do that right then.

"He scoffs at authority," the director continued, "and does not follow the hospital dress code. Frankly, he is a blight on the wonderful staff of this institution."

"His patients love him, and Dr. Starzi seems to think very highly of him."

"Yes. Let's discuss Dr. Starzi." The older woman stuffed herself into the chair opposite Victoria's desk and motioned for her to sit as well. "As you are well aware, young lady, you are more to me than a talented colleague I've taken under my wing. You're the daughter I wish I'd had."

Victoria nodded. But knew full well her tenuous role as pseudo-offspring was contingent upon her working hard to meet the director's expectations, siding with her in all hospital matters, and following her 'suggestions' to the letter.

"And I envision you with a man who is smart and respected," the director went on, "above reproach. An exceptional conversationalist. Someone an ambitious, professional woman can be proud to have on her arm. The perfect asset when socializing with Administration and schmoozing the upper tier to court prospective benefactors. Play your cards right with a man like Dr. Starzi…" she wagged her index finger "…and you can be half of a major power couple."

One of the two reasons Victoria had encouraged his pursuit. The other being he'd make a wonderful role model and father figure for Jake.

The director clasped her hands in front of her buxom chest. "With his wealthy, thankful patients spanning the country, just think of the opportunities for fundraising."

"At this point," Victoria said, "neither gentleman is a candidate for my arm. If I may speak candidly?"

The director nodded. "Of course."

"You should know Dr. Karlinsky is the father of my son." There'd been no need to identify Jake's paternity prior to this point.

Not one to make rash decisions or comments, the other woman sat quietly, introspective. After a short time she reached out and covered

Victoria's hand with her own. "Many of us have a bad boy or two in our past. But I'm happy to report, as we mature and identify what course we'd like our lives to take, our taste in men becomes much more discriminating."

Kyle stared at Victoria, who sat on the other side of the sticky, white food-court table, sipping a diet cola, more interested in her straw wrapper than him. "Thank you for including me today," he said.

She spared him a glance, one of the few he'd been gifted with during their Saturday afternoon excursion. "Jake wanted you here, so here you are."

"I've never seen a kid so happy to shop for a baseball glove." And it made him feel a part of something special to be included in the excitement.

"He's been bugging me to play for a while." She dragged her eyes back up to his. "Thank you for treating him to the glove and the new sneakers. It wasn't necessary."

"It's the least I can do. By my calculation, I owe you a couple of thousand dollars in back child support." And so much more.

She concentrated on the long white paper strip, intent on folding it into accordion pleats. "You don't owe me anything."

"I knew you'd say that." Miss independent. "So I made this out to Jake." He handed her an envelope that contained a check for five thousand dollars. "Put it into his college fund." No doubt in his mind Victoria already had one started.

She looked at the envelope, didn't move to take it. For a few seconds he thought she might refuse. Then she said, "Thank you. That's very generous," and tucked it into her purse without opening it.

He hated the stilted conversation between them ever since the old bat who ruled the nurses had shown up and caught him and Victoria behind closed doors. "So what did the nursing director want?"

"Mr. Madrin stormed her office to make a formal complaint about me."

"That man deserves a—"

"She talked him out of it, and came to commend me, in person, for my handling of the situation."

The dictatorial woman moved up a few notches in Kyle's estimation. "That was nice of her."

Victoria flattened out the straw wrapper and began winding it around her index finger.

"Are you going to tell me what's bothering you?" he asked.

"Nothing's bothering me."

Her words came out too fast and high-pitched to be true. "How long is Jake's party?"

She glanced over at the arcade where they'd dropped him off ten minutes earlier. "Two hours."

"You want to get out of here? We can go to my place, it's closer." If he could just get her alone he knew he could get her to relax.

"I don't even know where you're staying."

"I'm renting a one bedroom in the big condo complex a few minutes from the hospital." A functional unit, nothing fancy, which suited Kyle. "You want to take a look?" To sweeten the offer he added, "There's a pullout couch if Jake ever wants to sleep over," knowing she'd want to check out his digs before allowing their son to visit.

She didn't respond to his invitation, just sat there looking up at him. "You know wearing jeans to work is against the hospital dress code, right?"

"That was random."

"So why do you do it? Acting the rebel in high school is one thing, but you're all grown up. Enough already."

So that's what was bothering her. "Answer me this. Does my wearing jeans impact my ability to do my job; does it affect my performance in any way?"

"No, but—"

"Have my patients, your staff, or Dr. Starzi complained I lack professionalism? Have any of them taken issue with the care I provide while in my jeans?"

"No, but—"

"Come on." He held out his hand. "I'm not going to waste the brief time we have together talking about work. Jake's safe, he's having fun. Let's do a lap around the mall."

"My knee's a little sore."

It'd been fine all morning, her gait even with no noticeable limp. Maybe it was the elastic support he'd given her, or the written home exercise plan, or the private PT he'd forced on her since seeing her swollen knee. Whichever, he didn't believe her knee was too sore for a slow, casual stroll. "I'll get you in for an MRI on Monday," he threatened. "I've already spoken with the tech. She said to call first thing in the morning and she'd give me an idea when she can squeeze you in."

Victoria actually blanched. "Fine." She smacked her hand on the table, the breeze blowing the straw wrapper to the floor, where Kyle stepped on it so she couldn't pick it up. "Let's go."

After weaving through the weekend crowd they entered the flow of foot traffic behind a couple, walking hand in hand, a young boy perched up on the man's shoulders. Kyle felt a pang of regret that he'd missed out on moments like that with Victoria and Jake.

"So, tell me," Victoria said. "Where did you go after you left and how did you wind up with a PhD?"

Happy to get some real conversation going, Kyle answered, "The morning after everything went down I got in contact with Milt at the garage to tell him what'd happened." Aside from Ali, who would hear the news from Victoria, and his sister who would find the note he'd left for her when she finally returned to their trailer, Milt had been the only other person who might care what happened to him. "He called around and found me a job out in Habersville." Three short, or long depending on how you look at it, hours from Madrin Falls.

"You know, after that night he refused to service any of my father's cars."

Milt, who'd lived in a double-wide a few trailers down the row, had been more of a father to Kyle than his own father. "He looked out for me, even made me promise to take a high-school equivalency exam within one month or he'd have me fired."

"Good for him," Victoria said.

"Anyway, I spent my days working and my nights partying." Getting drunk, venting his anger by brawling with equally inebriated idiots, and screwing dozens of nameless, faceless women in a futile attempt to exorcize Victoria from his brain. "After a couple of months," during which his life spiraled out of control, "I got into a car driven by a guy drunker than me. He drove us into a cement overpass." And had almost killed them both.

Victoria stopped and reached up to trace the

scar on his chin, her touch soft, caring. "That's where you got this."

The group of kids walking behind them split up and filtered past.

Kyle guided her to the railing overlooking the ground level.

"Concussion. Broke a few bones." Eight to be exact. Spent seven days in ICU, six weeks on a medical surgical floor, and three months in a physical rehab facility. "During rehab I had a roommate named Fig." Ryan Figelstein. Eighteen like Kyle. Also involved in an MVA, only he'd been the driver, and his "accident", Fig had confided one night, had actually been a suicide attempt. "We hit it off, made each other laugh through the pain. When his parents overheard I had no one to go home to, they arranged for Fig and me to be discharged together and took me in." It'd been the first time he'd felt a part of a real family.

"Come on, there's a chocolate store up ahead," he said and, with a gentle hand on her back steered her in that direction. "Anyway, Fig's father asked what I wanted to do with my life. After spending so much time in physical therapy

I told him I might like to try being a physical therapist. Next thing I knew I was enrolled in the same college as Fig on a full scholarship." When he'd questioned the scholarship Fig's dad had told him, *"You keep an eye on Fig and get him to stay in college until he graduates, and we'll call it even."*

"I got in good with a few teachers who'd received a research grant. They invited me to work with them. I qualified for financial support as long as I was working toward a PhD in physical therapy so I signed up. And here I am."

"I'm glad everything worked out for you." Her words sounded distant, almost sad.

Because while he'd been cruising through college, blessed by the generosity of others, she'd been giving up her dreams, struggling to survive and make a decent life for their son. Talk about trading places.

"I'm sorry," he said. "I didn't mean…" to carelessly recite how easy he'd had it for the past eight years.

"Don't be sorry."

But he was. Sorry he hadn't protected her well enough. Sorry he hadn't made any attempt to contact her or inquire about her. Sorry he'd unknowingly traumatized her their last night together and she still suffered from the after-effects.

At least that he could fix, without a doubt, but not as a training mannequin, at the disposal of a student. He wanted her to experience pleasure from his touch, not fear, to yearn for intimacy with him, not run from it. He wanted to drive her wild with passion, to give her the ultimate satisfaction, again and again, to make up for all the years she'd gone without. He wanted to make her crave him, the way he craved her. And once he accomplished that, he'd go after her heart.

Because, with each passing day, Kyle grew more convinced that Victoria was indeed, his "one". He looked forward to seeing her, talking to her, even fighting with her. He enjoyed discussing Jake and participating in family activities, like heading to the mall. She was a wonderful mother, had been a great girlfriend. He'd lost her once, would not let her go again.

"Oh, look," she said, and veered over to the window of the chocolate shop. As she stood, staring through the glass with a look of desire Kyle hoped to one day soon see directed at him, he ducked into the store.

He returned to find her right where he'd left her. He handed her a small white bag. "Here."

She gave a gasp of surprise, smiled, and peered inside. "Pecan turtles."

"Only two." If it were up to him he would have purchased a dozen, but back in high school whenever he'd treated her she'd always specified, "*Only two.*"

She placed her hand on his arm. "You remembered."

He remembered lots of things. How she'd sat with him and Ali every day at lunch, walked right past the brainiacs and her snotty, rich peers, despite taunts she was headed to the wrong side of the cafeteria. How she'd fought with Mr. Strich when she'd thought Kyle had received an unfair grade on his trigonometry mid-term. (And got the grade changed from a C to a B.) And how she'd skipped school, for the first time ever, to sneak off to his trailer when he hadn't shown up to class for three straight days. His telephone had been disconnected for non-payment at the time. Upon finding him delirious with fever, she'd dragged him to her pediatrician, demanded an appointment, then carted him to Aunt Livi's house to recover from his pneumonia.

Sick as he'd been, with the two of them doting on him, it'd been the best two weeks of his life.

Victoria bit into one of the candies, inhaled, let her eyes drift closed, then exhaled. The expression on her face was one of such joy he couldn't help but wonder when she'd last indulged in her favorite treat. From this day forward it'd be a weekly event. When she slid the second half between her lips all Kyle could think about was making her replicate that look when they were alone and naked.

And to further his quest to make that happen, he needed more opportunities to entice her. "I want to show you something." He started to walk and she, licking her fingers, fell into step beside him. They'd passed the destination he'd had in mind earlier, but he didn't dare suggest they enter with Jake.

CHAPTER SEVEN

VICTORIA stopped short when she saw the store they were headed toward.

"I think I'll wait out here," she said. It'd make her the ultimate hypocrite to patronize a store she'd signed a petition to keep from opening.

"Don't go getting all prissy." He tugged her along. "Give it five minutes. If you don't like it, we'll leave."

Rock music blared through speakers almost un-identifiable in the dark-painted ceiling. Incense, at least she hoped that's all it was, permeated the air. Black T-shirts screen-printed with celebrities she didn't recognize lined the walls. Hundreds of novelties and gag gifts were displayed on huge shelving units. She walked past one display containing play handcuffs, fang tooth inserts, and fake blood, then another holding breast mugs with nipple spouts and realistic looking penis spoon rests, to stand in front of a display of colorful lava lamps. Out of the corner of her left eye she saw Kyle talking to a blonde-haired salesclerk. The girl smiled up at him, removed an elastic bracelet from her wrist, and handed it to him. She slid her eyes to the right to see a high-school-aged girl trying out an actual stripper pole. That's it. Probably only a minute had elapsed since she'd entered, but Victoria had seen enough. In the process of turning to leave, she halted when a synthesized cartoon voice sounded next to her left ear. "You're sexy."

She swung around to see Kyle holding a palm-sized, red gadget. He held it up and pressed a button. The voice said, "Are those real?"

People started to look in their direction. "Stop that." Victoria grabbed for it. Kyle held it up out of reach and pressed a different button. "Can I touch them?" A group of girls, standing close by, started to giggle.

Victoria couldn't help smiling. "You are going to pay for this." It felt fun to play. Frankly, she couldn't remember the last time she'd done it.

Seeming unconcerned with her threat, Kyle pressed another button.

"Pretty please?" the voice asked.

"Two can play at that game," she said, and grabbed for a similar-looking toy from the shelf beside Kyle. Holding it up, she pressed the top left button.

A different synthesized voice yelled out, "You're an asshole."

Victoria's jaw fell and her eyelids stretched so wide that if her eyeballs weren't anchored in her head, they would have dropped to the floor. "That's terrible." She threw the offensive voice box back into the basket with the others. "I'm out of here."

"Not yet." Kyle slid his arm around her shoulders and maneuvered her toward the back of the store. "All the good stuff is locked up." The moist heat of his breath singed her ear and sent a rush of arousing warmth surging through her.

"I've seen and heard enough, thank you very much." She tried to twist away.

"Two more minutes."

They stopped in front of a dark gray door. The red lettering on the sign that hung at eye level read: "Adult Amusements. Must be 18 or older to enter. See salesclerk for key."

"Ooh, no." She shook her head, stepped back

and bumped into Kyle. "I'm not going in there." Yet at the same time she wondered what illicit items the secret room behind the door held. Some of the books she'd read had touched on sexy board games, sex toys, and other bedroom… paraphernalia. Could they be so easy to obtain? One quick trip to the mall?

Kyle used the key on the elastic bracelet to unlock the door. When he pushed it open the overhead lights flicked on.

Victoria hesitated in the doorway.

"Try something new," he whispered in her ear. "No more living vicariously."

Right-o. It's what she wanted. At twenty-five years of age, it was high time she allowed herself to actually experience life instead of just reading about it.

"It's so small," she said, tugging on the neck of her sweater, hoping doing so would allow more air to enter.

Kyle coaxed her inside. "There's plenty of air," he said in a soothing tone. "I won't let you suffocate."

He didn't joke or tease. He was completely serious. And she appreciated that, especially when he closed and locked the door behind them. Despite her fear of tight spaces and the narrow isles stocked full of merchandise that made the small room feel even smaller, her curiosity urged her forward. Past feathered ticklers and wooden helping hands? Flavored body mousses and lotions, and edible bikini underwear? She picked up the box to take a closer look.

"If you put them on I'll eat them off," Kyle whispered in her ear as he walked past.

Maybe another time. Victoria threw the box back onto the shelf.

"Look at these." He called her over to a display on the far wall. "I'm told every girl should have one. Personally, I don't get the appeal."

He stood in front of a wall of vibrators. Her face heated. "I already have one."

"No way." He turned to her and smiled. "I can't picture it." And he looked to be trying rather hard. "You don't seem the type."

She wasn't. "A few months ago the pathetic state of my non-existent sex life became the topic of conversation at a girls' night out." And hadn't that been a totally mortifying experience since the decibels of Roxie's speech had increased proportionately to the number of beers she'd consumed. "The next morning I found an electronic gal pal on my desk along with a book about the elusive female orgasm."

He slid in behind her, placed his hands on her shoulders, and positioned her dead center in front of the display. "It's not a myth," he said.

So far she hadn't been able to prove otherwise. "So you say."

"Which one?" He asked his voice low, intimate.

She pointed to the model tucked away in a box in her closet.

"Do you ever use it?" He ran his tongue over the inner rim of her ear. It tickled, made the left side of her face tingle.

"Once." Sex with an inanimate object had turned out to be empty and unfulfilling and not at all for her.

He kissed down the side of her neck. Without considering the consequences, she tilted her head to give him better access. His hands slid down her arms, settling on her waist. He didn't crowd her, kept his touch gentle. His hands felt so good. "Did you like using it?"

She shook her head. He shifted his hands up her rib cage, stopping just below her breasts.

Darn it.

"You're going to like having me inside you."

But the last time...

"No. Don't stiffen up on me." He traced the outline of both her breasts at the same time, sliding up over sensitive nipples then back down again. "We'll take it slow. You'll be in charge." Up. Down. "Take only as much of me as you can handle." Up. Down.

It sounded perfect, but, "I don't know, Kyle. We're too different. We don't want the same things." And after giving it a lot of consideration she'd decided she wasn't the type of woman to engage in sex for the sake of sex. Once she found a suitable man who cared for her, whom she cared for in return, she'd share her issues and trust him to help her work through them.

"I want to explore your body," he said, his voice deep. "Learn what you like, what drives you wild. I want to give you pleasure, make you come." His palm grazed down her belly, the tips of his fingers sneaking beneath the waistband of her slacks. "I'd bet my life you want the same."

She wanted more.

He slid his hand further down, under the elastic of her panties.

Her mind knew she should stop him. Her mouth refused to convey the command, her hand wouldn't move to deter him.

"Do you want the same things?" His hand moved lower. "If you don't answer me I'll find out for myself."

A few inches and he'd find her wet and needy and ready to clamp down on his finger like a Venus fly trap to keep him from leaving her. She let her head fall back to his chest. "You have to stop, Kyle. We are at the *mall.*"

He smiled against her cheek. "I tried to get you over to my place." Without warning he slid a finger to her opening and sighed. "I knew it."

A battle raged inside her sex-starved body. The urge to tilt her hips to facilitate him sliding inside vs. a moral scream of outrage. She tilted her hips. He accepted her offer, the sensation foreign. Spectacular.

Within seconds he had her on the verge of something wonderful. "You need to stop." She circled his forearm with both hands and tried to lift his hand from her pants. "Please. I can't. Not here."

"Let me come over tonight," he pleaded, his voice rough. "I can ease your ache. You need me, and I need you, so much." As if to support his claim he pulled her back against his hard body. "You have to. We'll both die if you don't, then what will happen to Jake?"

Since there was no way to deny her attraction and retain any semblance of credibility, she opted for a version of the truth. "I'm not on birth control."

"I have condoms." *Now* he had condoms, when she was thinking clearly and rationally. She lifted his hand out of her pants and moved away. Feeling on edge, she tucked in her blouse with damp, shaky hands. "The last time I left a man responsible for birth control it didn't work out so well for me."

"I know," he said quietly, sincerely. "And I am sorrier than I can put into words for all you've been through. But I'm not sorry to have Jake. He's a great kid."

"He is."

"So…" He shoved both hands into the front

pockets of his jeans and did some rearranging. "Do you have any plans to go on birth control in the near future?"

Yes. She had a doctor's appointment scheduled for Monday. For a birth control shot, which, based on her cycle, should take effect immediately. But she told him, "No."

He cocked his head, studied her and smiled. "You know I could always tell when you lied."

"And what makes you think my going on birth control has anything to do with you? Are you so over-confident you can't fathom the possibility I made the appointment months ago?" She hadn't. Bottom line, Kyle's return and his effect on her body had compelled her to make the call. She simply did not trust herself around him.

His smile grew. "Go ahead and deny it, but we both know you want me," he teased.

"Sometimes I want to eat a pound of chocolate or skip a day of work," Victoria countered. "It doesn't mean I do."

"It's your call, sweetheart. Put off the inevitable if you must." He moved in close, set his lips to the outer rim of her ear, and whispered, "But know this, I am ready, willing, and, oh, so able, whenever you decide to give in to your urges."

The heat from his mouth sent tingles into her jaw and down the side of her neck. Her body, still aroused, fought the pull of attraction, the allure of all he offered. Gathering her restraint, she stepped back, not at all happy with his cocksure grin. Time to shut him down. "By the end of my date on Tuesday night I expect all my urges will be satisfied. But thanks for the offer."

No sooner did they clear the exit doors from the mall than Jake asked, "Can Dad come home with us?"

Victoria had had about all she could handle of Kyle for one day so she answered with an unequivocal, do-not-argue-with-me "No."

"But now that I have my mitt I need to get good at catching," Jake whined. "Daniel's been practicing with his dad for weeks. So has Jeremy. If I don't practice I'm gonna stink."

"And it will be all your fault," Kyle whispered to Victoria with a smirk.

"Okay," she growled. He could keep Jake occupied while she finished her homework.

Of course Kyle needed to stop by his condo to walk Tori and get his glove, which required even more time in his presence.

Jake was out of the truck and halfway to the stairs before Victoria even processed Kyle's invitation to check out his place. Tori met them at the door, happily rubbing up against each of them. "Hey, girl." Victoria massaged her behind the ears. After seeing the benefits of Tori's therapy, she'd grown to like the dog.

"Come on, Tor. Let us in." Kyle patted the dog on the butt and Tori ran back inside followed by Jake.

A discount motel room felt homier and more welcoming than Kyle's rental unit. It kind of reminded her of the neglected, downright dismal atmosphere of the trailer he'd once shared with his sister, which she'd only been inside the one time he had been too sick to deny her entry.

Most noticeably lacking were any personal items. Books. Pictures of family and friends. A favorite coffee mug or cookie jar. A colorful afghan knit by an aged aunt. At least it was neat. Orderly. And clean. "I love what you've done with the place," she teased.

"It has everything I need."

Perfect for the man who required no more than the most basic necessities. But sad. Who could possibly be happy living such an empty existence? Next chance she got she'd give him some of Jake's art projects to decorate the place, maybe a few pictures.

"That sofa pulls out into a bed," Kyle said. He glanced into the bedroom where Tori and Jake were busy playing. "In case Jake ever wants to sleep over," he added in a whisper.

She appreciated his discretion. Jake had mentioned sleeping at his dad's condo at least a dozen times in the past two weeks. But she wasn't ready to say yes. Not yet. The couch looked several decades old and well used since its manufacture. "We'll need to clean the mattress, dust the frame, and check for bedbugs," Victoria said.

Kyle smiled. "Of course we will."

Jake walked into the living room and asked, "Can we bring Tori home with us?"

"It's okay with me if it's okay with your mom," Kyle answered.

All three of them looked at her.

"Fine," she agreed. "But she stays downstairs."

"Goodie," Jake said. "Come on, girl." He ran to the door.

"Hold on," Kyle said, and walked over to grab a brand-new adult-sized baseball glove, complete with tags, from the dining room table. "Okay. Now I'm ready."

"That your glove?" Jake asked.

Kyle held it up. "When we went out to lunch last week you were so excited about playing baseball. On my way home I picked this up so we could have a catch together." He slipped it on and punched the palm area.

While Jake examined the glove and said "Cool" about six times, Victoria leaned against the wall, struck speechless by the thoughtful gesture, made after Kyle had spent a combined total of, at most, two hours with his son. It bespoke of him taking an active interest in Jake and wanting to be a part of his life.

"Come on, kid," Kyle said. "We're wasting daylight. You ready?" he asked Victoria.

"Sure." She followed them down to the parking lot. Jake chattered excitedly, holding onto Tori's leash. Kyle listened, squeezing in a response here and there when Jake took a breath. And Victoria walked behind them, all but forgotten. Until Jake asked Kyle, "Can I sit in the front seat on the way home?" And Kyle gave his standard answer, "It's okay with me if it's okay with your mom." And they both stopped and turned to her.

Well, of course it was not okay. Jake knew that. He was too small and barely out of his booster seat. "No."

"But, Mom, *Dad* says it's okay."

Call her naïve, but Victoria did not expect this play-one-parent-against-the-other routine, not from Jake. "You're not old enough or big enough to sit in the front seat, Jake, and you know it. I don't like you trying to take advantage of Daddy because he doesn't know all the rules yet. Now say you're sorry."

"Sorry, Dad," Jake said, looking adequately contrite, his expression changing to absolute jubilation when Kyle told him he'd be sharing the back seat with Tori.

Once home Jake and Tori ran off to play.

"I'm sorry about the front seat thing. I didn't know," Kyle said. "Give me a second to get over there. I'll help you down."

She opened the door and waited. "I can't expect you to know everything in two weeks." She tried to ignore the feeling of his strong hands on her waist and the enticing hint of cologne.

"Why don't you stay outside with us?" Kyle asked.

Victoria punched the code into the keypad by the garage door. "I've got work to do," she said. "And I don't have a glove anyway," she added with a shrug.

But knowing Kyle and Jake were outside, Victoria couldn't concentrate on her schoolwork. Instead she stood at her office window, watching them play in the yard. Envious. Kyle threw Jake the baseball, which bounced off the tip of his glove and rolled to Tori, who scooped it up in her mouth and ran. Jake dropped his glove and took off after her. Not far. Tori rolled onto her back, Jake rubbed her belly and she released the ball. Jake picked it up, said something and made a 'yuk' face. Kyle dropped his glove and chased Jake. Tori ran with them, jumping and barking, until all three wound up in a heap on the grass.

They wrestled around. Jake laughed and smiled with unrestrained joy. She hadn't seen him so happy since…never, could not recall him ever looking that happy with her. Because she always had so much to do, someplace to be, something to plan or worry about. And when they did play she tended toward educational games, always with his future in mind. Having Kyle around was good for Jake. For her? Not so much. He preoccupied her. Case in point—she looked down at the blank computer screen on her desk, her report guidelines and research papers still in her school folder. At the hospital she listened for him to arrive on the floor, waited with schoolgirl anticipation for him to visit her office. Why? So he could kiss her and proposition her and make her desire to act most improper? God help her. Yes.

Even at the risk of the promotion she needed to assure a stable economic future, Jake's attendance at the best colleges, and the chance for vindication. Validation. Which was why, from now on, she needed to be on guard to never wind up alone with him.

She sat down at her desk and fiddled with a pen. Then there were the niggling thoughts. Have sex with him. Get it out of the way. You'll stop thinking about it so much. If things turned out as awful as she feared, problem solved. He'd never bother her again and they could get on with co-parenting sans the underlying sexual tension between them.

But what if it wasn't awful? What if she managed to get through it without panicking and it turned out to be wonderful and loving and all she'd hoped for their first time? What would happen then? Could she incorporate Kyle into her ten-year plan? Would he support her goals and ambitions? Or derail her life plan? Again?

The basement door slammed.

Victoria walked to the top of the stairs. "Did you have fun?" she called down.

"Can Daddy help me finish my puzzle?" Jake yelled in response.

The puzzle they'd worked on together for weeks? He wanted to share the thrill of placing that final piece and the fun of the job-well-done dance with Kyle? Not her? It was only a puzzle, she told herself. So why did Jake's defection hurt so much? Why did she feel like an outsider with her own son, in her own home?

Before she could answer she heard Kyle say, "Sorry, champ I've got to run. There's someplace Tori and I need to be."

Where? Victoria wondered, but didn't ask. Kyle's life was none of her business. He could do whatever he wanted. With whomever he wanted. Made no difference to her. After she said her goodbye Victoria went into her medicine cabinet to take an antacid, hoping it would sooth the burning in her chest.

"Good afternoon, Mrs. Teeton," Kyle said when he entered her hospital room on Monday afternoon. "I hear you gained two pounds. Congratulations." He set a tin of chocolate-covered mints, apparently her favorites, topped with a big red bow, on her over-the-bed table.

She met his gesture with a tired smile. "Never in my fifty-four years have I ever celebrated putting on weight."

"Today is a day of firsts, like getting out of this room, for instance. You promised me and Tori a promenade."

"Nice segue."

"I'm a smooth operator."

A laugh that closely resembled Victoria's sounded out in the hallway.

"Are you ready?" he asked his patient.

Tori went up on her hind legs and placed her front paws on the bed beside Mrs. Teeton's shoulder. She reached over to pet Tori's head.

"No. I'm sorry. I'm going to have to cancel," she said. "I don't feel up to it."

A typical complaint in his line of work, but it was his job to keep his patients moving. "Then there's one more thing you should know about me," Kyle said a little louder than necessary, just in case Victoria was still listening. "I rarely accept no as a final answer."

"It's the truth," Victoria said, hustling into the room, going straight to Mrs. Teeton's closet and taking out her red bathrobe. "And he can be a real pest about it. It's best to just give in and save yourself the aggravation of having to deal with him."

"If only all women followed that philosophy," Kyle said, "I would live in a state of perpetual happiness."

Victoria brushed past him. She bent to whisper something in Mrs. Teeton's ear. The woman nodded. "Maybe you'll feel better once you get out of this bed," she said and, as efficiently as she did everything else, she slid the patient's legs over the side and assisted her into a sitting position. "Just sit for a few minutes." She kept her hands on Mrs. Teeton's shoulders to steady her. "The dizziness will pass."

"I can take it from here," Kyle offered.

"Can you really?" Victoria asked. "And just what do you know about getting a woman ready for her hallway debut?" She winked at Mrs. Teeton. "Give us a few minutes." Her expression serious, she added, "Maybe you can bring Tori to visit with Mrs. Madrin while you're waiting?"

When Kyle hesitated she tilted her head and mouthed, "Please."

"Sure thing," he said, and crossed over to the other side of the drawn curtain to find Mrs. Madrin lying on her side in bed, staring out the window.

"Excuse me, Mrs. Madrin. Are you up for a visit?"

Vacant eyes met his. "Do I know you?"

"You may not remember me but—"

"Hi, there, boy," she said to Tori, a hint of life returning to her eyes.

"She's a girl," Kyle clarified. "Her name is Tori. She's a therapy dog."

"Growing up I had a golden retriever just like her. Come here, girl." She tapped her hand on the mattress.

Tori, a notorious attention-monger, didn't wait for the command to proceed.

"Can she come up on my bed?"

Victoria answered from the other side of the fabric partition. "On top of the blanket, no pressure above your hips."

"Up," Kyle said in conjunction with the hand signal instructing Tori to jump onto the bed. Once there she turned in a circle, plopped herself at the foot of the bed and cuddled up against Mrs. Madrin's bent legs, setting her head on the woman's thigh.

Mrs. Teeton peeked around the curtain. A colorful scarf tied in a fashionable knot covered her head. Light makeup brightened her lips and cheeks. Victoria held onto her arm.

"I think Tori's tired," Mrs. Teeton said with a pointed look at Kyle. "Maybe she can stay with you while we walk?" she asked her roommate.

"I'd like that." Mrs. Madrin showed no emotion but continued to pet Tori.

Kyle glanced at Victoria who nodded.

"She's a good listener," Mrs. Teeton said.

"You can tell her anything and she won't repeat it," Kyle added, reciting the speech he gave each new patient. "Sometimes you need to say something out loud to hear how it sounds, before you're ready to share it with someone else."

Mrs. Madrin's eyes filled with tears.

"We'll leave you with Tori," Victoria said. "If you need anything at all, press your call bell and Ali or I will be right in." Outside, Victoria partially closed the door behind her. "Thank you," she said to Mrs. Teeton. "Getting out of that room will do you as much good as it will do your roommate to have a few minutes to herself."

"And thank *you*..." Victoria placed her hand on Kyle's arm and looked up at him with appreciation "...for loaning out Tori. I wanted to ask you before you went in there but I didn't see you arrive on the floor."

Because instead of stopping by her office to say "Hi," like he'd gotten in the habit of doing, he'd come down the other corridor, still angry and not ready to face her after finding out her Tuesday-night date was real, and she'd be spending it with Starzi.

"Shoot," Victoria said.

Kyle followed her line of sight to see Mr. Madrin and one of his assistants walking down the hall.

Without hesitation, Victoria intercepted them. Kyle listened, too far away to intervene, unable to leave Mrs. Teeton.

"Good afternoon, Mr. Madrin," Victoria said. "Your wife requires some privacy for the next ten or fifteen minutes. Feel free to wait in our patient lounge at the end of the hallway."

"Why? What's going on? What's happened?" Mr. Madrin made a move to walk around Victoria. She stepped to the side, effectively blocking the intimidating man's path on behalf of her patient.

She was one amazing woman.

"Please," she said to Mr. Madrin. "Your wife is in with our therapy dog."

Kyle liked her use of "our", like Victoria was comfortable with Tori being on her floor, confident in the service she provided.

"That's absurd. This is a hospital, not a petting zoo."

"Don't underestimate the power of animals to help in the recovery process," Kyle offered when he and Mrs. Teeton finally caught up to Victoria. "Animals are nonjudgmental. They don't interrupt or voice their opinions or make suggestions. They simply listen when someone needs to talk."

"Tori helped me tremendously," Mrs. Teeton added.

"We've tried everything we can think of to get your wife to open up about the accident, to discuss her loss," Victoria said. "So far nothing has worked. She barely eats and lies in bed staring out the window when no one's visiting. I refuse to give up until we find a way to help her. Our therapy dog, Tori, has a wonderful disposition and is extremely well trained. She is an asset to our staff and our patients adore her."

Victoria's words of praise for Tori made Kyle feel like a proud papa.

"Your wife's doctor approved Tori's visit," she said. "Your wife welcomed her."

Typical Victoria, checked with the doctor beforehand.

"I'm sure I saw her smile," Mrs. Teeton said.

"She…?" Mr. Madrin couldn't finish, overcome with emotion he turned away.

You could say a lot of negative things about the man, but he loved his wife.

"Please." Victoria took his hand in between

both of her own. "Go down to the cafeteria for a cup of coffee. Tori's handler, Dr. Karlinsky, is on the floor. And I will remain at the nurses' station in case your wife needs anything. If she asks for you I'll have you paged immediately."

Mr. Madrin placed his other hand on top of Victoria's. "I was wrong about you."

Most people were, mistaking her businesslike efficiency for a lack of caring, her superior intellect for a lack of compassion.

Victoria watched Mr. Madrin exit the floor then turned. "Whew. That went better than expected."

"Come on, handsome." Mrs. Teeton tugged on his arm. "I got all gussied up for our date. Are we going to spend it standing around doing nothing?"

"Absolutely not," Kyle said. "We're off."

A few hours later, almost finished with his chart documentation on 5E, Kyle watched Dr. Starzi strut onto the unit and cozy up next to Victoria outside the clean utility room. If this had been high school, Kyle would have been tempted to wedgie him up and leave him hanging from a hook on the door in the janitor's closet.

If there was any satisfying of Victoria's urges to be done, Kyle would be doing the satisfying.

"You're going to snap that pen in two and get ink all over the place if you don't lighten up," Roxie said, sitting down beside him.

"What's going on between the two of them?" Kyle asked, fighting the sick need to watch Victoria and Starzi together.

"He's shopping for a wife. Victoria caught his eye, meets his requirements."

"Does she have feelings for him?"

The pen did, in fact, snap, making a mess of Kyle's hand and the progress note he'd been writing. "Damn."

"Watch it." Roxie passed him a handful of tissues. "Or you'll have the profanity policewoman up your ass."

Kyle smiled.

So did Roxie.

"She's been alone a long time," Roxie said. "I think she likes Dr. Starzi, respects him as a physician. But she doesn't look at him the way she looks at you."

Hope surged inside him. "And how does she look at me?"

"Part puppy in a pet shop looking for some-one to take her home and love her, part woman stranded on a deserted island, devoid of male companionship for nine long years."

He checked to make sure Victoria didn't look at Starzi the same way. She didn't.

"Don't play with her," Roxie warned. "She doesn't look it, but she's fragile." She leaned in close. "If you hurt her I'll insert scalding-hot pokers into every orifice in your body. If you pull another vanishing act, I will make it my sole purpose in life to hunt you down and make you suffer in ways you couldn't imagine in your worst nightmares."

"Did you give Dr. Starzi the same warning?"

She waved him off. "He's harmless. You, on the other hand, hold the potential to break her heart."

"I won't." Not again. "And thank you," Kyle said.

Roxie raised her over-plucked eyebrows.

"For caring enough to threaten me."

"Don't disappoint." Roxie slapped him on the back. "Go win back your girl."

Oh, he planned to.

Two hours later, on his way to have a little chat with Starzi, Kyle headed past Victoria's office. As he neared her closed door it began to open. The director's voice said, "I don't know what you're waiting for, my dear. If you'd rather he not accompany you, he's not the man to build your promising future around."

Rather *who* not accompany her *where?* And whether the dragon lady liked it or not, Kyle was the only man Victoria would be building her future around.

The door opened fully and the director of nursing walked out. "Oh, look," she said when she spotted Kyle. "What prodigious timing."

Victoria walked into the hallway, looking ready to hurl.

"We were just speaking of you," the director said. "Next Saturday night is a dinner honoring several of our employees of the month. It's black tie optional. I hope to see you there," she added with false sweetness, and waddled away.

After she'd gone Kyle asked Victoria, "You okay?"

She nodded, took a deep breath, and sipped from the bottle of water in her hand.

"Why would I care about an employee of the month dinner?" Kyle asked.

Victoria scrunched her face. "Because I'm Miss January."

Kyle smiled at the centerfold image that flashed across his mind, Victoria draped across the front of a snowmobile, wearing nothing but a red and white striped ski hat and matching mittens. He blinked to clear it and focused back in on their conversation. "Then I wouldn't miss it."

He chose to ignore what looked more like uncertainty than happiness at his willingness to attend.

In the cafeteria Kyle found an empty table in the corner and waited. When Starzi entered he watched the little man fill a cup with coffee, add a splash of creamer and two packets of regular sugar. After he paid the cashier, Starzi scanned the tables until he spotted Kyle.

"You needed to speak with me?" Dr. Starzi pulled out a chair and sat down. "What's so important we couldn't discuss it up on the floor?"

"It's about Victoria," Kyle said. "And your date tomorrow night."

CHAPTER EIGHT

"Sorry I'm late," Victoria yelled as soon as she entered the basement. She slipped out of her shoes and hurried up the stairs. "I'll get dinner started in a minute."

"Take your time," Kyle answered from the kitchen. "Super-chef and I have everything under control. Dinner's almost ready."

What? Victoria stopped at the entrance to the kitchen and took in the wondrous scene before her. Jake, in gray sweatpants, his Superman T, and a red cape, stood on a chair in front of the stove beside Kyle. He had a spatula in one hand, a soup ladle in the other, and a chef's hat fashioned from paper towels on his head.

A warm contentment bloomed in her heart, circulated throughout her body. She smiled. Father and son, working together. Both so handsome.

"Go away, Mom," Jake said, spreading out his

arms, and trying to block the burners with his body. "You'll ruin the surprise."

"I'm not looking." She pretended to cover her eyes. "Thank you for picking him up," she said to Kyle.

"Anything I can do to help."

"Where's Tori?" she asked, hoping the dog wasn't curled up on a bed somewhere.

Through the spaces between her fingers she watched Kyle turn to face her. "In Jake's play-room. Go get changed."

Victoria had suffered a twinge of disappoint-ment when Dr. Starzi had cancelled their dinner date earlier that morning. She'd been looking forward to getting to know the man behind the doctor, to seeing if she could rouse up an attrac-tion to more than his high ambitions and out-standing work ethic. But seeing Kyle and Jake together, she realized there's no place she'd rather be than at home with the two of them.

After setting her briefcase in her office and changing into a jogging suit, Victoria returned to the kitchen. She knocked on the wall before entering. "May I come in now?"

Some urgent whispers and contagious giggles later Jake called out, "We're ready."

The small table in the kitchen empty, Victoria entered the dining room. "Very nice," she said, nodding in approval.

"I set the table myself," Jake boasted, and pulled out a chair. "You sit here."

He'd put Kyle in her seat at the head of the rectangular oak table and used Aunt Livi's good china, which she kept in the cabinet above the refrigerator. No way Jake had gotten to it without help.

She raised her eyebrows and slid a questioning glance to Kyle.

He shrugged. "The kid wanted tonight to be special." He placed his cloth napkin in his lap.

"Because it's our first family dinner," Jake said. "And me and Daddy cooked for you." He puffed out his chest proudly.

"Daddy and I," Victoria corrected automatically. "I love it." She kissed Jake on the cheek. "And I love, *you.*"

"Kiss Daddy, too," Jake ordered. "He helped."

Kyle extended his cheek in her direction and with a smile she kissed him, too.

"Now let's eat before it gets cold," Kyle said.

In the midst of an excited child who happily discussed his day and his father who listened intently and offered a high five for an A on a spelling test, grilled cheese sandwiches, tomato soup, and baby carrots never tasted so good. "Absolutely perfect," Victoria said, alluding to more than the food.

Kyle and Jake bumped fists then made a show of flaring their fingers on the pull-back.

"After dinner we have man-work to do," Jake said seriously, then slurped his last spoonful of soup.

"Not until your homework's done," Victoria said.

At the same time Kyle said, "After you do your homework."

They shared a smile.

"What do you have planned?" Victoria asked.

"Remember the p-r-e-s-e-n-t we talked about?" Kyle spelled out "present".

"What'd you get me? What'd you get me?" Jake slid off his chair and jumped up and down next to Kyle.

Victoria shrugged. "He's spelling at a fifth-grade level."

"What is it?" Jake asked again. "What's the thing we have to put together?"

Kyle looked at her.

She nodded her permission to tell Jake.

"A pitchback."

"A what?" Jake asked, scrunching his eyebrows together.

"Something to help you practice baseball," Victoria clarified. "If you're done eating, go get your homework," she said.

Jake ran to grab his backpack.

When Victoria stood to clear the table, Kyle stacked his dishes and stood, too.

"Thank you for dinner," she said. "You cooked. I'll clean up."

"I don't mind helping," Kyle offered, and followed her into the kitchen. "You wash. I'll dry."

Sometimes, during the long hours she spent alone, Victoria wondered what it would be like to share her life with a man, to have adult conversation around the dinner table and help with parenting's day-to-day responsibilities. How Jake would respond to welcoming a father figure into their little family. Apparently, if that man were Kyle, there'd be no problem at all. She soaped up and rinsed the first plate and handed it to him.

Having Kyle in such close proximity zapped her recently reawakened libido into full alert mode. Various body parts associated with procreation hummed to life.

Any time. Anywhere. Kyle's words tempted her.

She handed him the second plate. His arm brushed against hers. An enjoyable tickle shot from wrist to elbow.

Then Jake walked into the kitchen and asked, "Can Daddy help me with my homework?"

Kyle. He wanted Kyle to help him. Not her. Helping Jake with his homework was one of her favorite times of the day, the two of them totally focused on one another. She loosened her grip on a delicate bowl for fear she'd break it in two. This was a good thing. She rinsed the suds. After years on her own she now had help. She should be thankful. Accept it. Embrace it. Kyle hesitated, seemed to sense her turmoil.

"Go on," she said with a smile, hoping she'd achieved an air of indifference meant to cover her inner unrest. And as she finished the dishes she listened intently to the sounds coming from the dining room, in awe that Kyle could make even homework fun.

After Jake called out, "We're all done," Kyle entered the kitchen and held out the worksheets they'd completed together. "You'll probably want to check these over." He smiled.

He knew her so well.

"While we're outside we'll replace your basketball net. I picked one up while I was at the store."

There were some definite pluses to having a man around. "Thanks."

"Can I wear my tool belt?" Jake asked.

"You know where it is," Victoria said. Then smiled when, despite Jake's complaints, Kyle insisted he needed to wear a coat. Like a father, not a buddy.

Progress.

"And grab your glove," Kyle said to Jake. "When we're done we can throw the baseball around." He turned to Victoria and said, "Come outside with us."

"But you're going to do man-work." She smiled. "Male bonding over tools is not really my thing."

"It'll take fifteen minutes. Twenty tops. Promise you'll come out then."

"I have work to do." Between her job and school and the house there was always something that needed her time and attention.

"It'll keep for an hour. Come on. Have some fun with us."

She wanted to but, "I don't have a glove."

Kyle held up his index finger. "Are you saying if you had a glove you'd come out and have a catch with us?"

No. "It's a moot point because I don't have one."

"Wait right there." Kyle turned, jogged down the stairs and out the front door. A minute later he came back the way he'd left, carrying a bag from the sporting goods store. At the top of the stairs he handed it to her.

"What's that?" Jake asked, walking down the hall with his kid-sized tool belt around his waist, carrying his baseball glove in one hand and his coat in the other.

"Open it," Kyle said to Victoria.

She looked inside the bag. He'd gotten her a baseball glove.

"It's one you tried on when we were shopping for Jake," Kyle said.

She looked up at him. "You went back to the store and bought it for me?"

"So you could play with us," Kyle said.

It was truly the nicest, most thoughtful gift she'd ever received. "Thank you."

"Twenty minutes," Kyle said with a pointed look. "Promise?"

Victoria nodded, actually looking forward to it.

"Don't worry I'll get them," Jake yelled to Victoria when she missed the last of their six balls and it rolled across the yard to join the others.

"I catch like a girl," Victoria said, frustrated by her lack of skill.

"To catch like a girl you'd actually have to *catch* the ball." Kyle shot her a wink.

Victoria took off her glove. "I'm ruining your fun."

"Nah." Kyle wandered over to stand beside her. "I think we're ready to do something else."

"How about hopscotch?" Jake asked, running toward them, his jacket pockets stuffed with balls.

Kyle grabbed for his chest dramatically. "Say it isn't so." He stumbled to the ground. "My son plays hopscotch?"

"I'm good at it, too," Jake said undeterred. "I'll get the chalk." He ran into the garage.

"What's wrong with hopscotch?" Victoria asked. It helped Jake learn his numbers and improve his coordination. "It's not as easy as it looks."

"You're going to get the kid beat up playing that girly game."

"Don't be ridiculous." Victoria waved him off.

Jake came out of the garage carrying his bucket of multicolored chalk.

"Please tell me he doesn't play with pink chalk, too?" Kyle moaned.

"Knock it off." Victoria nudged his arm with the toe of her sneaker.

Kyle sat up. "I have a better game," he suggested. "Crime scene."

Victoria didn't like the sound of that one bit.

Jake did. "Cool!" He ran to Kyle. "How do we play?"

"Allow me to demonstrate." He flopped back on the driveway his arms and legs spread wide.

"Now outline me with chalk. You do the top half," he said to Jake. "Your mom can do the bottom."

Oh, goodie. She reached into the bucket of chalk, spotted one of her favorite colors and decided to have a little fun.

Unfortunately Kyle caught her. "No pink chalk." He rolled away. "What kind of television do you watch? The real cops outline the bodies in white chalk."

"Even I know that, Mom," Jake agreed.

And he did, in fact, have a white piece of chalk in his hand. "How on earth would you know something like that?" Victoria exchanged her chalk for a more acceptable color. Yellow. This time she hid it from view.

"When I go to Frankie's house," Jake said, "*his* mom lets us watch whatever we want on TV."

No more visits to Frankie's house.

"Stop yapping and start tracing," Kyle said. "It's cold down here."

Victoria started at his hip, moved the chalk down around his boot and up his inner thigh.

"You want to get in real close to the body,"

he said, challenging her, "so the drawing looks realistic."

She rounded the apex of his thighs, brushed the taut denim, saw movement beneath his zipper. She hesitated, watched, returned to his knee and started again. He shifted his pelvis.

"Come on, Mom," Jake said. "I'm done already."

She continued down the other side. "He's got long legs," she pointed out. Long, muscular, appealing legs. Stop it.

When it was her turn to play corpse, Kyle had no problem keeping tight to the curves of her body. So much so that she almost sent Jake inside to get her a drink so she could steal a kiss and feel his hands on her for real.

After each one had a turn, they traced each other in contorted positions and before long the driveway really did look like a crime scene. Victoria hoped for rain to wash it away.

Kyle looked at his watch. "Almost eight o'clock," he called out to Jake, who'd lost interest in Crime Scene and was chasing Tori. "Time to clean up and go inside." To Victoria's surprise she'd been having so much fun she'd lost all track of time. When was the last time that had happened?

Kyle showed her how to collapse the pitchback and while he and Jake carried it into the garage Victoria headed upstairs.

Outside the kitchen Jake asked, "After my shower can Daddy read to me?"

Victoria clamped both hands around the wrought-iron railing, hesitated and tried not to let her hurt show. Reading to Jake before bed was their special time together, to cuddle and wind down from the day. Having Kyle here was a novelty, that's all, she tried to convince herself. It's not like Jake preferred Kyle. Tomorrow night would be back to normal. She forced a smile. "Sure, honey." She reached down to flatten a rogue curl. "If that's what you want."

Kyle watched her. Understanding dawned. "How about your mom and I both read to you tonight?"

"Even better." Jake bounced on his toes and clapped.

"Meet you in the bathroom," Victoria said. She waited for Jake to ask for his dad to help him and felt an irrational, profound relief when he didn't.

"Thank you," she said to Kyle.

He placed his hand on her shoulder. "I know this isn't easy."

No. It wasn't. For so many reasons.

Half an hour later Kyle followed her out of Jake's room.

"I know I've said it before but he really is a great kid," Kyle whispered. "Helpful, respectful and eager to please. You've done an awesome job raising him."

His words came as sweet music to her ears, confirmation she'd done well despite her concerns she didn't spend enough time with Jake, was too strict, too serious. For some reason, praise from Jake's father meant so much more than she'd imagined it would. Moisture accumulated at the base of her eyelashes.

Kyle loosely gripped her arm, stopping her. "Thank you," he said with heartfelt gratitude. "For not getting rid of him. For all you had to give up to keep him. For raising him better than I could have done on my own." He turned her, lifted her chin, and looked deeply into her eyes. "You are an amazing woman, Victoria Forley." And he kissed her.

A gentle, sensual, wonderful kiss.

He wrapped his arms around her and twirled them into the kitchen, landing with his back to the counter. She pushed up against him, relished the evidence of his arousal. For her. And decided it was time. Tonight. With Kyle. They may not love each other, may not have any future together aside from raising Jake, but she cared for him and could tell he cared for her. More importantly she trusted him, believed he would be careful with her, listen to her.

"Remember when you said I could practice? With you? Any time? Anywhere?"

Kyle held her close, rested his chin on top of her head and said, "Yeah."

"How about tonight? In my bedroom?"

She braced herself to be scooped up and carried off down the hall.

Instead Kyle placed a hand on each of her shoulders and eased her away. "Are you sure?" he asked, totally calm and in control.

At her nod, he reached for her hand and quietly led the way to her room.

There was no mad dash to the bed, no heated frenzy to tear off each other's clothes.

Kyle locked the door. "Do you want the light on or off?" he asked.

"On," she said. "I want to see you." To survey every beauty mark and muscle and hair follicle.

He smiled and walked toward her.

Surprisingly, she felt more excited than nervous. Eager. Ready.

"There's something I want to try. But first..." She reached for the hem of his T-shirt and asked, "May I?"

He tilted his head in agreeable fashion and like they were attending high tea and she'd asked for a taste of one of his sweet cakes he answered, "Please do."

His chest bare, she ran her fingers over the hills and valleys of his beautiful physique, set her cheek to his soft, warm skin and inhaled his scrumptious masculine scent.

He brought his arms around her and gently caressed her back.

"I like this," she said. This closeness with a man. With Kyle.

"Me, too," he agreed.

But she wanted to give him pleasure, needed to prove she could do it. With her hands leading the way, down his sides to his hips, she dropped to her knees, looked up, and smiled at his look of surprise. "Okay?"

"Sure, but..."

She unsnapped the button of his jeans, shutting him up, then eased the zipper down over his growing erection. Excitement fizzed inside her. She slipped a finger under the elastic waistband, freeing him, and lowered his underwear and pants together.

Kyle stood perfectly still, his magnificent erection pointing due north. As a nurse she'd seen hundreds of naked men over the years. But none had made her want like this one. She reached for him, suffered a moment's hesitation, remembering—*No, not like that. When Leanne does it she...*

Big hands surrounded hers, eased her on to his heated flesh. "Like this," he said, showing her what he liked.

For something so big and hard his skin felt remarkably smooth.

Kyle expelled a breath. "Damn."

She let the curse slide.

Remembering a scene from one of her favorite novels, Victoria took him deep into her mouth.

Kyle moaned.

Eyes closed, head tossed back, his look of absolute enjoyment thrilled Victoria. She retreated, relished the feel of him inside her mouth. When she reached the tip she swirled her tongue and took him deep a second time.

Again he moaned.

Victoria's confidence grew. She loved this power to control his pleasure, to go at her own pace, to make him come. And she set to work doing just that.

Kyle kept his eyes closed for fear the sight of Victoria on her knees at his feet would be too much. Lord help him, he couldn't remember any woman arousing him more.

He clasped his hands behind his butt to keep from coming on too strong, controlling her or scaring her. But, damn, if she kept it up he was in real danger of coming embarrassingly quick. He needed to think about something other than her moist lips and soft tongue and hot mouth.

Twenty-six bones in the foot.

She sucked him deeper. He fought the urge to thrust into her, his control growing fickle.

Calcaneus. Talus. Navicular.

She gripped him with both hands, moving them in tandem with her mouth.

Medial cuneiform. Intermediate cuneiform. Lateral cuneiform.

"Am I doing this right?" she asked, sounding frustrated. "Shouldn't you be gripping my head or telling me how good my mouth feels on you?" She looked up at him. "Maybe moving a little, like you're enjoying yourself?"

He almost laughed out loud, but didn't, although it was touch and go for a few seconds. "Is that what the men do in those trashy books you read?"

"They're not trashy." She pouted. "And yes. They do. If I'm doing something wrong, you need to tell me."

"Baby." He slid his fingers through her short hair. "You are doing everything right." Any more right and he'd be basking in post-orgasmic bliss. "I'm trying to be on my best behavior since you're new at this." Wait a minute. Could she possibly have developed such skill solely from reading romance novels? "You are new at this, aren't you?"

She nodded. "Pathetic, isn't it?"

"It is light years away from pathetic." It was exciting yet humbling at the same time. "And for the record, you've pushed me to the edge so quick I feel like a teenage newbie."

Still on her knees, she looked away. "It's not the same when I have to ask you to say it."

Leave it to Victoria to give him a hard time during a blowjob.

"I'm sorry. I've ruined the mood," she said. "Maybe you should go." She started to stand.

Nothing short of a five-alarm fire with flames posing a direct threat to them or Jake could make him leave her bedroom right now. He placed his hand on her shoulder, halting her movement. "Honey, I bet we can get it back in under a minute." Under fifteen seconds.

"You think so?"

"I'm certain."

Not one to back down from a challenge, Victoria took him back into her mouth. And yessiree, he'd been correct. "You see what you do to me?"

Cuboid. First metatarsal. Second metatarsal.

He cupped the back of her head, careful to not make her feel forced in any way. And, Oh. My. God. His vision went blurry. A delicious pressure started to build.

So good. Too good. But when Victoria set her mind to something there was no stopping her. And, frankly, he only half wanted to.

The urge to come was too powerful to stop. "I'm going to…" was all he could choke out before a deluge of frenzied lust took over. His hips moved of their own accord. His knees weak, his mind a haze of ecstasy, satiated perfection.

Heart pounding, lungs heaving, Kyle felt like he'd just finished a full marathon. Totally spent. Drained. He reached out a hand to steady himself against the wall,

"Wow," Victoria said as she stood and bent to brush off her knees. "I did it."

"Yes, you did. And I'd like to check out a few of those books you like to read." He pulled her against his chest and kissed the top of her head. "Give me a moment to rebound and I'll do *it* to you."

"Yeah. About that." She pushed away, looking

suddenly nervous. "It's getting late." She faked a yawn. "Maybe another time."

Like he'd let her go that easy. "Give me fifteen minutes. Let me make you feel as good as you made me feel."

"Fifteen minutes. You are a fast one." She fidgeted with her watch. "But if it's all the same to you, I'd rather not rush." She looked everywhere but at him. "I'm thinking we'll need at least an hour. Maybe two."

In a perfect world.

He hated to see her distressed, but if he had any hope of helping her conquer her fears, of making her comfortable with his touch and rekindling an intimate relationship between them, he couldn't let her run from him any longer.

"Come here." He kept his voice quiet, held out his hand palm up. Inviting, not commanding. She needed to come to him on her own. And he was prepared to wait as long as it took.

"I may not be able to…"

"You will," he said, confident he could give her the ultimate satisfaction.

"What if I have a panic attack?"

"You won't."

She flung her hands to the sides and cried out, "How do you know?"

"Because we are going to take it slow, and you decide how far we go." He kept his voice calm. "We're going to talk the entire time I'm touching you. I'll tell you what I plan to do before I do it, and you'll tell me what you like and don't like." He wanted to step toward her, meet her halfway. He didn't. "You're going to tell me if anything I do makes you even the tiniest bit uncertain or uncomfortable, and I will stop immediately. I won't let you go back into that closet." He cheated and leaned, just a little. "I want you right here, with me, in the present, the entire time."

Kyle understood. He'd always had an uncanny ability to figure her out, to burrow to the root of her moods, identify the catalyst then soothe with affection or diffuse with distraction and humor. In their short time together he'd grown to know her better than anyone else, and it seemed he still did. He held out his hand to her. An offer from a caring friend, a boy she'd once loved, a man she trusted to help her through the next fifteen minutes.

She took it.

He blew out a relieved breath.

"I like it when you kiss me," she said.

He smiled and gave a little tug. "Then let's start with that."

Victoria walked forward, her head tilted, up her lips ready.

His kisses disarmed as much as they enchanted, made her want, no need, more. She looped her arms behind his neck and held him close.

"I need to sit," he said against her lips. "Come." He shifted them toward the bed. "Straddle my lap." A marvelous idea. But once settled into place she realized he'd be holding up their combined weights with nothing to support his back. "This can't be comfortable for you."

"Honey, I could be sitting with my bare butt on a block of ice and be perfectly content as long as I had your body right where it is."

Good. Because she liked their current position, she rocked her hips along his length. A lot.

"I want to see you," he whispered, and reached for the zipper of her jacket. He waited for her to nod her agreement before he proceeded to lower it.

Then with the care and skill of a seasoned artisan handling delicate gold leaf he divested her of her clothes until he had her naked from the waist up, giving her a play by play of everything he planned to do before he did it.

"You're beautiful," he said with the perfect amount of reverence. "I'm going to kiss you now," he said, then listed the spots he planned to show some attention. Her neck, collarbones, breasts and nipples tingled at their mention.

At the end of his titillating journey, Victoria ached for him to shift his focus to the empty, throbbing place inside her, to fill her and make her whole. As if he could sense her need, he slid his hands below the elastic of her sports pants, palmed her butt cheeks, and pulled her against him as he undulated beneath her.

"I can feel your heat through my jeans," he said, his breath coming in harsh pants. "Tell me you're ready. Tell me you want me." Keeping up his assault down below, he ducked his head and kissed her.

At that moment fear and uncertainty were distant emotions, a protective safety zone of arousal and desperate yearning keeping them at bay.

"Please," she said. "Make love to me. Like this. Just like this."

"Take off your pants," he said. Not a command, a plea.

Done. She had her remaining clothes discarded before he'd fully unzipped his jeans. So she helped him.

"Hold on." He pulled out his wallet and took out two condoms.

"A-plus for positive thinking," Victoria said. "But one should be sufficient."

He smiled and pushed his briefs and pants to the floor. "We'll see." Her mouth watered at the glorious sight of him, as he rolled on a condom and returned to the bed.

"Come."

With that goal in mind, she climbed back onto his lap, the feel of him between her legs making her weak with desire.

He moved his hand, stroking and circling, around where she wanted him, closer, almost there, before moving away.

"Tease," she said.

Totally serious he told her, "I need to feel you. Please."

She nodded, fought the urge to clench around him as his fingers slid in and out of her primed body easily. Spectacularly.

"My God." He dropped his head onto her shoulder and trembled. "You feel so unbelievably good." With that pronouncement he removed his hand, placed it on the bed behind him and leaned back. Waited.

Now it was her turn. *You feel so unbelievably good.* She could do this, would do this.

"Kiss me," Kyle said, leaning forward just enough for their lips to meet. She sank down on top of him, lifted then lowered herself again, each time taking a little more of him into her body. He stretched her, but where the first time there'd been discomfort, this time she simply felt a sublime fullness, the best possible kind of full.

He kissed down the side of her neck. "You okay?" he whispered.

Better than okay. "Yeah."

He groaned. "You have no idea what you're doing to me."

Then he pushed in the rest of the way, shifted beneath her, and she felt it. The connection she'd hoped for all those years ago, the melding of body and soul, the binding of two people in love. And part of her loved him still. His caring nature at work and with Jake, his commitment to being a good father, and his ability to spark her to life with the simple act of entering a room. They were different. She ambitious, he content. She stressed, he carefree. She serious, he fun. But they complemented each other. Was that enough to build a relationship on? To try again? Did she even want to? Did he? Or was this nothing more than sex between two old lovers? A one-time therapeutic, guilt-easing joining to absolve him of the past?

"What are you thinking about?" he asked.

"Nothing," she lied, picking up the pace, determined to finish.

Kyle groaned, the sound empowering.

She moved fast, liking the ability to control his pleasure.

"That's it," Kyle said. "Just like that. And if you care for me at all, you will not stop again."

Victoria settled into a rhythm that had Kyle's breath coming in pants. Before long her breathing matched his.

"Lean back and put your hands on my knees," Kyle said.

She did. And the next time he surged deep a solar flare of wonderfulness shot off inside her. "That was…" he hit the same spot again "…so…" The third time her cry of completion joined his and she would have collapsed to the floor if Kyle hadn't caught her.

Holding her against his chest, still inside her, Kyle fell back on the bed, bringing Victoria with him. He hugged her close and kissed the top of her head. "That was…amazing."

And the magnitude of the moment hit. She'd done it. Had sex. Amazingly great sex. Without panic or fear. She lifted her head and looked at Kyle through blurry eyes. "Thank you," she said, unable to control her emotions. "Thank you." She collapsed onto his chest and cried.

"Honey," Kyle said. "What's wrong? Shhh." He caressed her back. "Please, don't cry."

Relief and satisfaction and utter contentment at being in Kyle's arms sent her to a tranquil place. "I didn't think I could do it." She let her eyelids drift closed, completely relaxed for the first time. "Thank you for showing me I can."

"With me," he said, then tightened his hold on her. "Only with me."

At some point, Victoria couldn't pinpoint exactly when, Kyle must have tucked her into bed. She awoke to him snuggled in behind her, his hot, naked body pressed to hers, and for a few minutes imagined Jake was someplace else so she could spend the entire night in Kyle's arms, every night in Kyle's arms, every minute.

Good Lord, stop it. She opened her eyes. She was not some infatuated teenager. She was a woman with responsibilities and a ten-year plan, a woman who would not lose focus on her goals because of a man. No matter how yummy that man turned out to be or how right it felt to be cuddled up next to him.

CHAPTER NINE

KYLE never understood a woman's desire to cuddle after sex. He did it to make them happy, but got the heck out of there at the first opportunity. So why did he hold Victoria in his arms, her back molded to his front, worried if he let go they might never share this closeness again?

Because she'd been ripped away from him once.

"Are you awake?" she asked.

"Yeah."

"About the employee of the month dinner."

"That mind of your never shuts down, does it?"

"Not often. And not for long." She lifted the hand she held and kissed his palm. "You don't have to go if you don't want to."

If you'd rather he not accompany you, he's not the man to build your promising future around.

"If you're going to be there, of course I want to go." He hesitated. "Unless you'd rather I didn't."

A tense silence ensued.

"You know it's black tie?"

Was that all that was bothering her? "I seem to recall the nursing director mentioning that."

"You know what that means, right?"

"I don't live under a rock. Of course I know what it means." He kissed the back of her head. It wouldn't be the first penguin-themed affair he'd attended.

"I figured the last thing you'd want to do on a Saturday night is dress up in a tux."

"True." He cuddled her close and nibbled her ear. "I'd much rather be dressed in my birthday suit."

"Cut it out," she said, and smacked his arm playfully. "I'm worried you're going to have a terrible time."

Probably. "But you'll make it worth my while afterwards, won't you?"

"I'll do my best." She rubbed his thigh. "Shoot. I forgot. I'm on the planning committee so I'll have to be at the dinner two hours early. Would you mind meeting me there?"

"That'll give me some extra time to work on the little surprise I have planned for you." He'd been thinking about it since finding out about the upcoming affair.

"A surprise?" She partially turned onto her back to face him. "Will I like it?"

"That's the plan."

"What is it?"

"I'll never tell," he teased.

She turned to face him, well, his chest anyway, and reached her hand down between them. "I bet I can make you."

Damn, she was a fast learner. "Feeling confident?" He rolled onto his back. "Give it your best shot."

As successful as her attempt had been, it wasn't enough to get him to share his secret then, or any of the other times she'd tried over the next week. But he'd sure enjoyed her efforts.

Kyle looked in his rearview mirror, straightened his black bow tie and grabbed the corsage from the passenger seat.

He ignored the looks of disdain from a snobby older couple, the white-haired man dressed in a perfectly cut tuxedo and the white-haired woman wearing a full-length fur coat, and, head held high, pulled open the door to the hospital's catering hall and entered the den of vipers.

The first person he saw was Mr. Wheeton, owner of Wheeton's Pharmacy. Kyle fought the urge to confront the man, remembered the helpless anger of being accused of stealing condoms, being restrained and having to deal with the cops, when he'd done nothing wrong. Mr. Wheeton had said nothing to the well-dressed boys who'd actually stolen them and had laughed at Kyle's predicament on their way out of the store. Even though a humiliating search of Kyle's clothes and backpack had turned up nothing, Mr. Wheeton had not apologized, and he'd barred Kyle from the store anyway.

Mr. Wheeton, who had not aged well, looked Kyle over and nodded in approval, obviously not recognizing him. Teenage Kyle would have shot him the finger. Adult Kyle simply turned away without acknowledging him. This was going to be a long night.

He entered the ballroom and spotted Victoria right away, talking to a group of women beside the dance floor. Rather than approach her, he decided to take a few minutes to savor the beauty of the striking, knee-length red satin dress that showcased her fabulous figure and enjoy the anticipation of being the envy of every man in this room once he took her into his arms.

At least he'd thought so until she noticed him and charged in his direction, looking ready to engage the enemy in battle. "How could you do this to me?" She glanced from side to side and dragged him into a quiet corner. "I specifically told you this is a black tie affair, and you show up in jeans? What were you thinking?"

He pointed to his brand-new black bow tie. "I am wearing a black tie." He waited for her to notice his snazzy new black suit jacket and $100.00 dress shoes.

If she did, she didn't mention them.

"You think this is a joke? Some sick joke?" Her eyes widened in horror. "Is that the same black T you wear to work every day?" She made it sound like he only had one and hadn't washed it. "You couldn't even buy a nice dress shirt? Why, Kyle? Why tonight of all nights?"

She sounded frantic. Her breathing sped up. She was really upset. "Whoa, honey." He reached for her. "Calm down."

She twisted away. "Calm down?" she asked loud enough to attract the attention of two couples standing nearby. "Calm down?" she asked, again, even louder. "My father is here," she snapped. "I haven't spoken to him in over eight years. I haven't seen him in over two. And he's here. Tonight. In this very room."

Kyle went on guard, scanned the crowd. "Did you know he was coming?"

She clutched her fist to her chest and inhaled deeply. "No, I didn't know he was coming. He's on the board of directors but he's never come to a dinner before." She looked Kyle up and down. "And you, my date, show up looking like the troublemaker you were in high school."

"This is not as big a deal as you're making it out to be."

She stiffened and narrowed her eyes into angry slits. "It's a big deal to me. You have no idea how long and hard I've had to work to earn the respect of the people in this room," she said in a curt whisper. "And the first date I bring makes a mockery of the formal nature of the affair."

"You're joking, right? You were born into these people, you *are* these people."

Had her eyes been swords, he'd no doubt have two lengths of steel penetrating his brain. "You mistake me for the girl you knew in high school, before I got pregnant and had my previous life stripped from me," she said tightly. "Almost everyone in this room knows me as a nurses' aide who went to community college, someone who benefited from the hospital's scholarship program. I don't have a fancy degree from a prestigious university to recommend me. I have worked and networked and, yes, kissed butt, and I am on track to become the youngest director of nursing in the history of Madrin Falls Memorial Hospital. And how do you think my skeptics will view my ability to manage a three-hundred-bed facility when I can't even manage my date?" She glanced around. "Perfect. Everyone's staring at you."

Only a few people, and probably due to her carrying on more than his attire. "They're staring at you because you're the prettiest woman in the room," he said to pacify her. "Here." He handed her the corsage.

"You got me a wrist corsage? Made of daisies?"

"Your favorites." Apparently not anymore because she held the plastic carton like it contained a dead lizard.

He took advantage of her silence to explain. "You missed your senior prom because of me. I thought maybe we could pretend tonight is prom, you know, recreate the magic, and…" he held his hands out to the sides "…this is what I would have worn. I could have rented a tux and showed up like the rest of these yahoos, but then the night wouldn't have been special."

"It would have been special for me," she pointed out. "So this is your big surprise?" Well, yeah. Recreate prom. Show up with a corsage. Dance too close. Maybe sneak outside and steal a kiss beneath the stars. And right about now she was supposed to be in his arms, telling him what a wonderful idea it was and how much she appreciated the thoughtful gesture.

He waited.

The MC took the microphone and directed everyone to take their seats.

Victoria didn't move.

The director of nursing walked over and looked Kyle up and down in her usual disapproving way. "Is everything okay over here?"

Victoria held her corsage behind her hip, out of view. "Yes," she said. "Fine."

"Come," the director said. "Let's find our table."

Our table. Kyle had an ominous feeling the night, which started off teetering precariously close to the edge of disaster, had just been pushed into its depths.

"Kyle was just leaving," Victoria said. "He only came to drop off…"

What? He couldn't believe his ears. His outfit embarrassed her to the point she'd rather toss him aside than be seen with him? And without a crumb of appreciation for his attempt to make up for her missing prom? At that moment, Victoria epitomized everything he'd rebelled against. Fine. She wanted him gone, he'd go.

Unfortunately, before he could escape, the director threw a beefy arm around his waist and anchored him in place. "Nonsense," she said, then turned to Victoria. "You're an honoree, dear. You must be accompanied by a date."

Exactly where was that written?

When they reached their table the director said in her booming voice, "Ladies and gentlemen, may I present our lovely Victoria's date, Dr. Kyle Karlinsky."

A hush fell over the table and a few of the surrounding tables as men and women checked him over with disapproval. Unfazed, he plastered a fake smile on his face and pulled out Victoria's chair. She stood so stiffly he half expected to hear a crack when she sat down and bent to hide her purse and the corsage he and Jake had designed specially for her under the table.

As the MC droned on, his voice an irritating buzz in Kyle's head, he drifted to peruse the crowd, recognized his pain-in-the-butt high-school principal, the stodgy mayor, and Victoria's father, whose eyes shot poisoned darts of contempt in his direction.

Acting cool, while his body shifted into fight mode, Kyle slid his left arm around the back of Victoria's chair and lifted his beer in a toast to him. Intense hatred flared in the man's eyes.

The swallow of brew that followed did not go down easily.

Kyle's life had come full circle, landing him under the scrutiny of the societal elite who'd judged and condemned him in his youth, who despised him as much as he despised them. Only tonight Victoria stood among them. And while he couldn't care less what the others thought, Victoria's opinion mattered. He should have realized how important this night was to her and dressed the part, not focused on his need to make up for the past. Stupid. Stupid.

When Victoria took the small stage she looked radiant, poised and genuinely pleased. To her apparent surprise, before letting her sit down, the MC read three letters of praise for Victoria and her staff, the last from Senator Madrin, then handed her the microphone. In response she gave an impromptu speech that was both succinct and impressive, and held the audience rapt. Kyle watched, with pride, the ease with which she engaged the crowd and earned their adoration. She belonged up there, a polished speaker, a born leader. The director beamed as if she'd birthed Victoria herself. Victoria's father focused on his daughter. Proud. Bereft. He tossed back a shot of what looked like whisky.

After being ignored through the ceremony, Kyle leaned in to apologize over salad. "I'm sorry."

"It's okay." Victoria smiled politely.

But it wasn't, a fact she made all too clear each time she refused his request to dance.

As if their tablemates picked up on the discord between them and took it as a personal affront, they made little effort to include him in their conversations, which suited Kyle just fine. He hated judgmental idiots who formed opinions about a person based on their attire or where they lived. Screw them all. He had nothing in common with these people and could not wait to leave.

He took a swig of beer, open bar the only bright spot of the evening.

"Well, well, well. If it isn't the happy couple," a familiar voice slurred behind him.

Victoria went rigid.

"You did great up there, honey," her father said. "Then you sat down next to this hoodlum and lost all credibility."

"Please don't do this, Daddy," she pleaded, looking down at her plate.

Kyle calmly placed his napkin on the table and stood. "Why don't we take this outside, sir?" he suggested.

Victoria's father swayed on his feet as he turned

his enraged eyes on Kyle's. "Back to claim the prize, huh, gutter rat?"

"Nothing can stand in the way of true love," he answered quietly, then leaned in and added, "Not even a bogus rape charge."

Victoria pushed back her chair and stood. "How could you?" she asked her father, the hurt in her voice provoking a physical pain in Kyle's gut.

"Figured that out, did you?" Her father laughed, the sound pure evil. "Well, it served its purpose well enough."

"And what purpose was that?" Kyle asked. A dangerous rage gathered strength. "Breaking your daughter's heart? Controlling her life?" A concentrated loathing oozed and boiled in his core. "And what kind of father disowns his child when she needs him most? Leaves his daughter and grandson to struggle?"

The old man still had some muscle on him because he pushed Kyle back into the table hard enough to send glasses flying. Something shattered. A woman shrieked in alarm. The chatter around them came to a halt. Kyle knew he should stop, walk away, but he couldn't, the opportunity to make her father pay for his heinous acts, for manipulating *him*, making him miss out on eight years of his son's life and separating him from the only woman he'd ever loved, too appealing to pass up.

"She'll always be too good for you," the other man spat. "Look in the mirror. You'll never measure up, never be man enough to deserve her."

"That's not true." Victoria stepped between them. "Kyle's a PhD. He's doing a fantastic job at the hospital. He's a wonderful father to Jake."

"His illegitimate son."

Victoria recoiled, glanced at her father then at the surrounding crowd in absolute horror and humiliation.

Kyle imagined how good the crunch of Mr. Forley's eye socket would feel against his knuckles. Fists up and ready to do damage, Kyle stepped forward. Time for Daddy to pay for his sins.

"He's an embarrassment." Mr. Forley moved his hand up and down as if displaying Kyle's faults. "A low-class nothing. Look at him, ready to brawl like a common street thug."

"I like it better when you ignore me, Dad," Victoria said, sounding tired. "You've had too much to drink. Let me find you a ride home."

Kyle tried to sidestep around her so he could wipe that smug—

"Stop it." She flung her arm out to stop him and glared up into his eyes, determined, her body trembling with anger. "If you don't walk away this instant I swear on my mother's grave I will take Jake in the middle of the night and you will never see either of us again."

They were almost at her house, without one word uttered between them, when Kyle pointed to Victoria's lap and said, "You should put that on. Jake helped me pick it out." Which made her feel even more terrible.

She opened the plastic container, the sound unexpectedly loud in the quiet car, and slipped the elastic band onto her wrist. "Thank you," she said quietly. "For the flowers and pretend prom. It was sweet." But she'd been too blinded by panic at seeing her dad for the first time in years and disappointment over Kyle's apparel choice on such an important evening to acknowledge it until now.

"Just not the right time or place," he conceded.

"No," she agreed.

"Jake and I thought daisies were your favorites."

She stared out at the shadows of the passing landscape. "Because he picks them for me." Like Kyle used to whenever they'd visited their special spot by the lake.

"Do you have a favorite flower?"

"Roses. Look, I'm sorry for giving you a hard time. When you said you had a surprise I assumed you'd rented a tux. I got all pumped up to show you off and introduce you around. Then Dad showed up and I thought, even better. Let him see firsthand how he'd misjudged you, how well you turned out."

"And the only way you could be proud to show me off, the only way to prove I turned out well, was if I showed up in a tux?"

He made her sound like a superficial snob. Maybe she was. "It shouldn't matter, I know," she said. "But it does." Especially now when she had so much riding on the professional reputation she'd spent years cultivating, which after tonight probably equaled the value of one pair of contaminated disposable gloves.

He drove down her driveway, parked next to Roxie's car, and turned off the ignition.

"Goodnight," she said, hoping to end it at that.

"I promised Jake I'd come in to tell him about our night."

"Fine." Victoria slipped out of the truck and jumped down without waiting for him to assist her. Five minutes, that's it. Then she needed to figure out how to salvage her career after the airing of her past in a room filled with people pivotal to her advancement at the hospital. And distance herself from Kyle.

It was going to be a long, sleepless night.

But evaluating, planning and strategizing got pushed to the back of her mind upon first glimpse of the mess that greeted her in the hallway outside Jake's playroom. Victoria felt on the verge of bursting into flame.

"What do you think, Mom?" Jake asked, bobbing on bare toes that peeked out from beneath his pajama pants, his fingers clasped together, an elated smile on his face.

"I think you should be in bed." She spoke to Jake but glared at Roxie, who held up both hands in surrender.

"You said you'd be home to kiss him good-night," Roxie said. "He was concerned if he got into bed he'd fall asleep and miss it. You know I have trouble saying no to the tyke."

Victoria scanned the haphazard piles of toys and stacks of books lining the downstairs hall-way. "Obviously."

"Ah, well," Roxie said with a swift swivel toward the stairs. "Gotta run. Work tomorrow. Want to get a good night's sleep so I'm ready to give it my all bright and early." In thirty seconds tops she collected her things and closed the front door behind her.

"Why?" Victoria asked, standing in the door-way of Jake's emptied-out playroom.

"Me and Roxie were talking," Jake said, cautious, his eyes wide, recognizing she was not as happy about his surprise as he'd been a moment earlier.

"Roxie and I," Victoria corrected automatically.

"That it didn't make sense for Dad to live all by himself when we have room for him to live here," Jake continued.

Roxie had better hope Victoria forgave her by

Monday or she'd be assigned to narcotics count, crash-cart check and the night shift for a month.

"I said he could move into my room, but me and Roxie…" Jake stopped. "I mean, Roxie and I decided Dad was too big for bunk beds."

If she hadn't been so at odds with him, the thought of Kyle's big body hanging over a top bunk might have brought a smile to her lips.

"And you need your office to do your work, Mom."

"So you cleaned out your playroom to make a place for me to stay," Kyle said.

Would this nightmare of a night ever end?

Jake's excitement returned. "The couch turns into a bed, and we left you the TV and some movies."

Kyle knelt down and opened his arms, his sincere appreciation for Jake's thoughtfulness evident. "Come here."

With a great big smile Jake ran to his dad, jumped at his chest, and clamped his arms around Kyle's neck. "That's the nicest thing anyone has ever done for me." Kyle hugged him tightly and kissed his cheek.

"It's time for bed," Victoria said. Time to take back control of her life.

"Can Daddy tuck me in?"

Another toothpick to the heart. "Not tonight, honey," Victoria said.

"But we have to talk about guy stuff," Jake begged.

"Your mom said no, Jake." Kyle sounded stern. Fatherly. "We can talk tomorrow."

Jake cupped his hands around his mouth and asked in a stage whisper, "Did she like the flowers?"

"She loved them," Kyle answered.

Victoria looked down at the pretty white petals. "I did," she said. "I do. It was so nice of you and Daddy to buy them for me."

Jake stood in the hallway, the disappointed, argumentative face that usually preceded one of his infrequent meltdowns looking up at her. Victoria could not handle one more confrontation this evening so she gave in. "Oh, go ahead," she said to Kyle. "Five minutes," she stressed to Jake, holding up five fingers for emphasis.

"Yay! Come on, Dad," Jake said. And Kyle followed him up the stairs.

Victoria had just poured a cup of herbal tea when she heard Kyle emerge from Jake's room. She didn't move, had hoped to be safely locked away in her bedroom before he left.

"You okay?" he asked from the doorway.

Was she okay? Whoever said, "There is no such thing as a stupid question," had been wrong. "You mean for someone who's lost any chance at the promotion that was the foundation of her ten-year plan? Or someone who may find herself searching for a new job next week? Maybe someone who's going to have to explain to her son why he has to go to a state school because she can't afford a private college?" She dunked her tea bag so aggressively water splashed onto the counter.

"It's not as bad as all that," Kyle said from directly behind her.

"Oh, no?" She turned on him. "You have psychic powers?" She held out her palm. "Please. Give me a reading." Her anger started to escalate. How dare he minimize the magnitude of this evening's events? "Tell me when I can expect to be offered the director's job. Make sure to take into consideration the stigma of teenage pregnancy. Oh. And the fact my date to a major hospital function, the father of my son, a man who is already on the outs with the director of nursing—the woman who gets final say in her replacement and holds control of my future—for rebelling against the hospital dress code, showed up in jeans. Oh. And here's the best part. Are you ready? And then gets into a public altercation with the hospital's chairman of the board."

"Your father is chairman of the board? Hell."

"I couldn't have said it better myself." Victoria thrust her palm at him, purposely poking her fingers into his chest. "So go ahead. Give a look. Exactly when can I expect the promotion that will finally give me the financial security I need to ensure my son's future? My guess is one week after never," she yelled.

"Calm down," Kyle said. "You're going to wake Jake."

"I'll calm down after you leave." Hopefully. Maybe after a hard run on the treadmill for an hour.

"I'm not leaving until you calm down."

"You're the one making me crazy," she screamed.

Like an absolute lunatic. She dropped her head and let out a breath. "I'm sorry."

"Come, sit at the table," Kyle said, reaching around her to pick up her cup. "Talk to me. Tell me why this job is so important to you."

Thinking maybe it would help him understand why she needed to put the kibosh on their budding relationship, Victoria sat across from him at the tiny two-person table, looked into her tea, and began. "For the first seven years of Jake's life we struggled. After Aunt Livi died, no matter how many hours I worked or how much I economized, there were weeks all we had to eat was macaroni and cheese or peanut butter and jelly. I gave Jake terrible haircuts and limited him to the small box of crayons, which I made him use down to the nubs, and sent him to daycare with yard-sale finds because I couldn't afford the cool toys his friends had. And even though he never complained, I felt ashamed I couldn't do better."

Kyle reached out and touched her arm. "I know you said what I would have done doesn't matter," he said. "But I swear on everything I hold dear, if I'd known about the baby I would have worked two jobs, three if needed, to provide for you both.

I would have gone to the labor classes and parenting classes and happily helped you take care of Jake. I most definitely would not have left you to deal with being pregnant and raising a child on your own." He reached for her hand and took it in his. "I wish I'd known. I wish I could have been here to help you."

"I appreciate that." She slid her hand from his. "But you weren't here. It's been just Jake and me for five years now, and he is the most important person in my world. Seeing to his needs, ensuring I can provide him the best possible opportunities for his future are my top priorities." She blew on her tea and took a sip. "I will never revisit that desperate time in my life. For as long as I live I will see to it he never has to go without another day in his life."

"You're not alone anymore." Kyle squeezed her forearm. "You can count on me to help you in any way I can, to share the financial load. You don't need to chase after some high-profile job that requires you to suck up to self-important, judgmental egomaniacs."

Victoria sat back in her chair she hoped out of reach. "When I was little I thought I could count on my mom to be there to take care of me and love me every day. And she died when I was five. I thought I could count on my dad to always be there for me, but he disowned me when I made a decision he didn't agree with. I thought I could count on Aunt Livi for a safe haven, but she died and left me worse off. And I'd thought I could count on you until you disappeared without a word for almost nine long years." She couldn't keep the bitterness from her voice. "The only person I know, without a doubt, I can depend on is me."

"I get it. You have no reason to believe me," Kyle said. "But I'm not going anywhere."

"Regardless of whether you're a part of our lives or not, I need to be financially independent, to know I can support myself and my son. That I'm prepared for him to enter the college of his choice and grad school or medical school, whatever he wants." She took a sip of tea.

"To do that I need a high-paying job," she continued. "The director of nursing job. And I will do whatever it takes to get it." Even carve the man she was starting to love out of her life because he didn't mesh with the image she needed to project to upper management and the board of directors.

"Tell me something," Kyle said. "What's so special about the director of nursing position at Madrin Memorial? Someone with your drive and determination could easily make more money doing any of a dozen managerial positions at a larger hospital."

But if she left town no one would see her success. Her father who'd given up on his pregnant daughter, convinced keeping Jake would ruin her life. All the kids at school who'd teased her, the valedictorian too stupid to use birth control. All the adults who'd criticized and lectured her, the wealthy girl, giving up a promising future to enter the ranks of unwed teenage moms.

"This is where I live, where my friends are," Victoria explained. "But I want that job for the financial security it will provide as much as for the chance to prove to the people of this town that I am smart and capable, not stupid for getting pregnant so young. I want the challenge and prestige and respect that comes with it. I enjoy getting dressed up to attend fancy dinners for fundraising and networking." Now for the kicker.

"And I want the man in my life to accompany me as an asset. Not a liability."

Kyle showed no reaction. "So that's all I am? A liability?" he asked, calm as can be.

She swallowed. Hated to say it, but, "Tonight, at the dinner, yes. And as long as you buck hospital policy and loathe the very people I'm trying to impress, I can't be with you."

"Let me get this straight," Kyle said. "Getting that promotion is more important to you than me?"

It'd been her goal since she'd first stepped into the hospital as a nursing student eight years ago, something to strive for and look forward to and feel positive about.

Unable to look at him, she stared into her tea. "Over the years I've given up so much. I refuse to give up my goal to achieve the top nursing spot in the hospital." And for the final blow. "After Jake, it's the next most important thing to me."

"Then I guess that's it." Kyle placed his hands on the table, pushed back his chair and stood. "The last thing I want is for you to lose out on one more opportunity because of me. But I'm

Jake's father, and I'd like to be able to spend time with him every day."

"We're adults. I'm certain we can figure out an arrangement that works for both of us."

Without another word, Kyle left, slamming the front door with a finality that brought on the terrible ache of loss, the emptiness of feeling totally alone and the tears that accompanied both.

CHAPTER TEN

KYLE spent a good part of his Sunday on the somewhat smelly green couch in his living room, with Tori, reflecting on his past, thinking about the future, and missing Victoria and Jake. The book he'd tried to start, one he'd been eagerly awaiting from the library, lay closed on the coffee table. It didn't hold his interest. The quiet emptiness of his condo taunted him, the stark contrast to the activity and warmth of Victoria's home, the grim reality of life devoid of family.

He'd done it again. Walked out on Victoria without so much as a thumb wrestle of resistance.

What was wrong with him? Why hadn't he pointed out that her getting the director's job and them being together didn't have to be mutually exclusive? That he loved her. And if he needed to dress different and try harder to impress her colleagues and business associates, he would do whatever it took to make her as proud to be with him as he was to be with her.

Not that any of it would have mattered. Because, after all Victoria had been through, she wouldn't believe his promises. He'd need to show her, to prove himself with actions rather than words. The realization had him sitting up so fast Tori jumped off the couch and started to bark.

"Quiet down, girl." Kyle rubbed her back. A plan started to take form. And after taking Tori outside for a quick walk, Kyle took a trip to the mall.

"Three more," Kyle said to Mrs. Teeton early Monday morning.

Lying on her back in her hospital bed, his patient tried to straighten her left leg while he supported her calf and applied a moderate level of resistance to the heel of her foot.

"Why do you insist on torturing me day after day?" she asked with a grunt of exertion.

"Resistance exercises are for muscle strengthening. When we first met, three weeks ago, you couldn't get out of bed by yourself, now you're able to walk the hall independently."

"The way you've been pushing makes me think you want to be rid of me."

"I want you safe and able to take care of yourself when you return home tomorrow. Now the other leg." He held out his hand and she bent her right leg and placed her heel against his palm. "Speaking of which, I sat in on your discharge planning meeting. Four more. Come on. You're almost done."

Mrs. Teeton finished her reps. Kyle lowered her leg to the bed and brought the covers up to her waist.

"Thank the Lord that's over with," she said, just as she did at the end of every bedside PT session.

"I hear your boyfriend wants to take you home and you're refusing him," Kyle said. "Like you've refused his visits since you've been in the hospital."

She wouldn't meet his eyes. "This is none of your business, Doc."

Kyle pulled a chair next to her bed and sat down. "I'm making it my business. The man obviously cares about you. According to the nurses, he calls in daily to check on you. He wants to take care of you and help you."

"That's the problem," Mrs. Teeton said tears forming in her eyes. "I don't want to be a burden." Kyle handed her a tissue. "He took care of his wife for two long years before she lost her battle with cancer. He's such a sweet man." She blotted at the inner corner of each eye. "I don't want him to have to go through that again."

"It's what people do when they love someone," Kyle said, realizing it's what he'd do for Victoria without a moment's hesitation.

"Not that it matters. One look at me…" she ran her hand over her bald head "…and he'll run in the opposite direction."

Kyle took a trifold paper out of the folder he carried with him. "Here's another pamphlet from a woman who sells wigs made from real hair. Call her this time, tell her what you want, and she'll stop by the hospital with some options first thing in the morning."

Mrs. Teeton opened the advertisement. "How do you think I'd look as a redhead, Melanie?" she asked her roommate.

Mrs. Madrin walked over to Mrs. Teeton's bed, Tori walking beside her. "I think you'd make a beautiful redhead. And I can call my husband's secretary to bring over an assortment of cosmetics that will get rid of those dark circles and play up your beautiful blue eyes."

Tori had bridged the gap between the two

women, who had become very close over the past few weeks.

"A little blush on your cheeks," Melanie continued, "and some color on your lips and he won't be able to tell you're sick."

"But I am sick." Mrs. Teeton dropped the pamphlet to the floor and closed her eyes. "And I have months of outpatient chemotherapy before Dr. Starzi will know my fate."

"It's not about the time you have left," Kyle started.

"It's what you do with your time," Mrs. Teeton finished.

"Your boyfriend sounds like a nice man," Melanie said.

"He asked to meet up with me tomorrow morning so I can teach him your exercise plan." Kyle bent to pick up the pamphlet and placed it on the over-the-bed table.

"Don't you dare," Mrs. Teeton warned.

"It's that or I coordinate in-home physical therapy, where someone like me will visit you three times per week."

"Heaven help me. There's no escape, is there?"

"You've made so much progress. I won't take

a chance on you backsliding after discharge," Kyle said.

"Let Dr. Karlinsky teach your boyfriend your exercises," Melanie coaxed. "And let that sweet man take you home. I've heard so much about him, I just have to meet him."

Mrs. Teeton lay there quietly with her eyes closed. Kyle and Melanie waited. After a few minutes she whispered, "Okay."

Kyle set his hand on the blanket covering his patient's thigh. "I know that wasn't easy, but I think you made the right decision." He'd had serious concerns about her not eating or exercising and winding up right back in the hospital within a month if she went home alone.

"Oh, she did, she definitely did," Melanie said, looking happier than he'd ever seen her.

"I hear you're going home tomorrow, too," Kyle said to Melanie.

"Well, they couldn't keep one of us here without the other," Mrs. Teeton said.

Melanie reached down to pet Tori. "Thank you for giving my husband the information for Tori's breeder. He promised to get me a dog just like her."

Kyle held out his hand to Melanie. "It's been a pleasure getting to know you. Good luck."

Melanie shook his hand, looking near tears. "Thank you. Tori has…"

"Yeah." Kyle leaned over and patted Tori's side. "She's a good girl."

"I'm off. I will see you…" he pointed to Mrs. Teeton "…tomorrow morning."

"Not too early," Melanie said. "Her boyfriend can't see her until after her wig arrives."

"I'll tell him eleven o'clock."

With a quick knock on Victoria's open door, Ali walked into her office. "Did you see Kyle? Dang, he cleans up good."

Like she always knew he would. But even she'd been shocked by his transformation. Charcoal-gray dress slacks, a white button-down shirt, and a tie. A tie.

Kyle's barber had sheered the swag of bang that partially obscured his handsome face, opening it to full view, while leaving plenty of short, thick waves in the back. Perfect for a woman to run her fingers through. Victoria had come close to suggesting he wear a hat lest the site of him trigger a rash of gotta-catch-me-that-man hysteria among the available women at the hospital. Unless that's what he was going for now that he knew there was no chance for them to be together.

The burn in her chest worsened.

"For as good as he looks," Ali said, "he's walking around here with a big old storm cloud over his head. One that looks remarkably similar to yours."

"Leave it alone, Ali," she warned her friend.

Who didn't listen. "Is it because of what happened at the dinner? You know, your father deserves a good punch in the face, and after what you told me about that sham of a rape charge, I think it's fitting for Kyle to be the one to do it."

"I'm not talking about this," Victoria said, scanning a computer printout on her desk, pretending interest on some random page.

"He loves you. Any fool can see it."

The words blurred.

"And you love him, too, although you're too stubborn to admit it."

"Hello, ladies," the director of nursing said from the doorway. "I hope I'm not interrupting."

Victoria blinked to clear her vision before looking up. "Of course not." She stood. "Come in. Ali was just leaving."

"I see you've finally brought that man of yours up to snuff," she said, waiting for Ali to slip out before walking into Victoria's office. "I had no doubt, if it could be done, you'd be the one to do it."

Victoria did a double take. Had the director really just said what she thought she'd heard? Because to date, the woman had given no indication she thought Kyle was at all redeemable.

The director closed the door.

Would there ever come a time when she didn't feel the need to seal Victoria in her office to speak with her? "He's not my man," Victoria clarified, taking a sip of water from the bottle on her desk, in desperate need of an antacid. "And I'm sorry about Saturday night. I promise it will never—"

"Oh, pish-posh." The director waved her hand shoo-fly style. "That's the most excitement we've had at a hospital event in years. I bet our June dinner gets more interest because of it." Which would benefit the hospital since the quarterly dinners also served as fundraisers.

Glad her family problems were good for a boost in attendance.

"Don't look so conflicted, dear." The director handed her several letters. Some handwritten, the one on top typed. "On award night I highlighted excerpts from Senator Madrin's letter, focusing on the sections that pertained to you. But he also mentioned Dr. Karlinsky. It seems *your man* came in after hours to visit with his wife and give her time with Tori. Mr. Madrin credits that as a major facet of her recovery."

Why had no one on her staff mentioned his visits?

"In one short month, he's accumulated seven complimentary letters."

After seeing Kyle in action at work, it didn't surprise her. He didn't go about doing his job in a grandiose manner, like Dr. Starzi. He didn't seek praise or recognition. He simply did what needed to be done, and more, in his unassuming, low-key way, quietly earning the respect of his patients and co-workers. He got results. He made a positive impact on the lives of his patients and their families, and in the end that's what mattered. Not what he wore or what Administration or anyone else thought of him.

And she'd been too blinded by her need to succeed to recognize his true value.

"I wanted you to know," the director went on, "I will be nominating him for April employee of the month. Close your mouth, my dear. That look is most unappealing."

Victoria did as instructed.

"I hope it's enough to entice him to take the staff position he's been offered, because even with the positive response to his dog, I cannot abide that animal walking the halls of this hospital. At Friday's meeting to discuss the continued presence of his pet, my vote will remain a steadfast no." The director locked eyes with Victoria. "And I expect your allegiance."

"Of course," Victoria responded. She always sided with the director. But she'd never disagreed with her mentor's course of action.

Until now.

And since she had a personal stake in the outcome of this particular matter she would need to go out of her way to handle her decision on how to proceed delicately and objectively.

Someone knocked at the door. "I'm in a meeting," Victoria called out.

The door opened the slightest bit. "I'm sorry to bother you," Nora said, "but your 'do not disturb' button is on, and Jake's school is on line one. It's the principal. He says it's urgent."

When Victoria arrived home she went straight to the freezer to make Jake two fresh baggies of ice for his eye and lip. "I don't understand why you wouldn't tell the principal who did this to you," she said, swallowing down an intense urge to retch at the sight of her baby's battered face, the skin around his left eye an angry, swollen red, his upper lip cracked and puffy, and the rim of each nostril crusted with dried blood.

"It's over. I don't want to talk about it," Jake said, his words muffled behind an icepack.

"It most certainly is not over," Victoria said, handing him the fresh bags of ice, each wrapped in a paper towel, and tossing the melting ones into the sink. "Not until the person or persons responsible are punished. Now, come, sit down." She pulled out a kitchen chair for him. "Talk to me. Tell me what happened."

"No."

"No? You're telling me no?" She crossed her arms over her chest. "That is absolutely unacceptable, Jake Forley. If we don't give the principal at least one name, what's to stop any of them from hurting you again?"

"He won't."

"He? So it was one boy." Good. That was a start. "Was it someone from your class? Did anyone else see what happened? And where on earth was your teacher while you were being beaten?"

"Stop it, Mom."

"I will not stop it, young man. Not until you give me this boy's name. And his parents are notified and he is reprimanded."

"No," Jake yelled. Panicked.

"Honey." She sat down on the chair across from him. "Are you worried this boy will get angry and hurt you again? Because let me assure you, when I'm finished at that school he'll be lucky to be accepted back into class."

"You can't go down to school. I promised."

"Who did you promise?"

"Why do you make everything a big deal?"

Jake jumped off his chair and threw his bags of ice on the table. "I hate you. I want Dad. Only Dad."

His verbal missile landed dead center in her chest. The result: catastrophic. The aftermath: complete devastation.

Jake ran down the hall. A door slammed.

All Victoria could do was breathe. Her sweet son, the most important person in her life, hated her for trying to protect him, for doing her job as a mother.

I hate you.

I want Dad.

Only Dad.

She inhaled. Exhaled. Moved her arms and legs to get the circulation flowing. She could handle this.

Gathering up the bags of ice, she stood and walked to Jake's room. She knocked. No answer.

She opened the door to find Jake, lying on his bed, facing the wall. "Honey, you need to keep this ice on your face to keep down the swelling."

"No."

"Come on, Jake."

"Go away," he yelled. "I want Dad."

"Well, Daddy's not here. I am. And I want you to—"

"I don't care what you want."

Bam. The hurt just kept on coming. Inhale. Exhale. "Are you in pain?"

No answer.

"What would you like for dinner? I can make soup or—"

"I'm not hungry."

"You will be later."

"No, I won't," Jake yelled.

Victoria stood in silence, couldn't move, appalled by her son's behavior. After a minute or two Jake asked in a small voice, "Did you call Dad?"

"Not yet."

He started to cry. Tiny sniffling tremors quickly turned into heart-wrenching sobs that shook his small body.

"Oh, honey. No. Don't cry." Victoria hurried to the bed, sat beside him and rubbed his back.

"Can I…have his phone…number…so I can… talk to him?" he asked in between choppy breaths.

"Of course you can." Victoria leaned in to kiss the back of Jake's shoulder. "I'll write it down for you so you can call him any time you want. But let me get in touch with him this time. I'll do it right now. Promise. I'll ask him to come over as soon as he can. Okay?"

Jake nodded.

"I love you," Victoria said.

Jake sniffled in response.

Late Monday afternoon the 5E staff was abuzz about Victoria, running out of work early with no explanation. If anyone knew why, they weren't talking. Kyle went about his business, visited two patients, and tried not to worry. If something'd happened to Jake she would call him. Wouldn't she? His cellphone vibrated in his pocket.

He stood to retrieve it, looked at the screen and opened a text message.

From Victoria: "Please come over. ASAP. Jake needs you."

Kyle punched his timecard, left the hospital, and was in Victoria's driveway in thirteen minutes. With a stern "Stay", he left Tori in the truck.

He ran up the front steps, whipped open the screen door and knocked. After waiting what he thought was a reasonable amount of time considering the circumstances, maybe two seconds, he tried the knob and pushed open the door.

"Victoria?" He climbed the stairs.

"In here," she answered from the kitchen, where she sat at the small square table with a mound of shredded napkin strips in front of her, half meticulously folded into tiny accordion pleats.

She looked up at him with sad, exhausted eyes. "Jake got beat up at school today. And before you say anything, I checked with the teacher. He was over by the swing set when it happened." She stared out the window and added quietly, "Not playing hopscotch. Or using pink chalk."

"Is he okay?"

She nodded.

The tightness in his chest eased. "It's not your fault," Kyle said.

Victoria looked down at the table and returned her focus to folding. "I can't be sure because he wouldn't tell me or the principal what happened. It turns out he hates me and only wants you."

That didn't sound at all like Jake. What the heck had happened? "Is he in his room?"

"Yes. I think I heard him packing." A tear made

its way down her cheek to her chin and dripped onto the table. "You can't have him," she said. Another tear followed the path of the first. "He's all I have and I won't let him go."

"Ah, Vic." Kyle knelt beside her. "I'm sure this is all a big misunderstanding. Let me talk to him and see what's going on."

Victoria took his hand and squeezed. "Thank you for coming."

"I'm here for both of you. Any time. Always."

With a kiss to her palm he went to knock on Jake's door.

"Go away," Jake yelled.

Kyle walked in. "That's some greeting, kiddo," he said.

Jake rolled over. "Dad."

It took a significant amount of self-control not to react to his son's bruises. "So what's got your mother all upset?" Kyle asked, keeping things laid back, ignoring the suitcase by the foot of Jake's bed.

"Mom's mad I got beat up at school," Jake said.

Understandably. "You want to tell me what happened?"

"Only if you promise not to tell anyone."

"If you don't want me to, I promise I won't."

Jake sat up in bed and Kyle sat down beside him.

"The other week, a kid in my class tried to copy my answers on a big spelling test. I raised my hand and told the teacher. It wasn't the first time and he got in trouble." Jake looked away. "After that he wasn't in class for a bunch of days. I thought he got kicked out by the school. But when he came back he said his dad got real mad at him so he was real mad at me." Kyle leaned in and whispered, "He had a cast on his arm. Do you think his dad broke it?"

"I don't know. I hope not." But he intended to look into it.

"Today the kid's brother, he's a fifth-grader, snuck out of lunch when he saw my class on the playground. He said his brother got beat because of me so I deserved to get beat."

Violence bred violence. "No child deserves to get beaten." Kyle caressed Jake's uninjured cheek with a loving hand, the only way he would ever touch his son.

"After the fifth-grader ran back into the school the kid in my class said he was real sorry and begged me not to tell. He said if his brother got in trouble then their dad would beat him even worse 'cause he's older. I don't want anyone getting beat up because of me," Jake said with a shudder. "I've seen their dad and he's big and scary-looking."

Now it all made sense. Jake wouldn't reveal a name out of concern for the *bully's* safety. Kyle couldn't be prouder, but trying to protect children from an abusive parent was an awfully big undertaking for an eight-year-old. "Why didn't you tell your mom what you told me?"

"She got all crazy and wanted me to tell the principal so the kid's parents got told. She would have made a mess of everything."

"Well, she's not crazy anymore. Now she's mostly sad because for some reason she thinks you hate her."

Jake dropped his head into his hands. "I didn't know what else to do to make her stop. She kept asking and asking. I'm sorry."

"It's not me you need to tell. It's your mom," Kyle said. "And while we're at it, those two boys sound like they have it pretty bad at home."

Jake nodded.

"Like they need help."

He nodded again.

"And who better to make sure the school helps them than your mom? She'll make sure they do it."

"Or she'll nag them and nag them." Jake smiled.

"I say you tell Mom. And then we talk about what we can do to see those boys don't get hit by their dad again. I bet she'll have lots of ideas."

Jake thought about it for a minute and said, "Okay," then added, "And, Dad? I don't like getting beat up. Will you teach me to fight?"

Kyle didn't want his son following in his confrontational path. So he said, "I have a better idea. Give me a few minutes with your mom then we'll come in and discuss it. Okay?"

Jake climbed onto his lap and wrapped his arms around Kyle's neck. "I love you, Dad." The words danced through his mind and cavorted with his skin cells before settling in his heart. A contented warmth spread throughout his body. Kyle held Jake close. He was responsible for this child. To love him, care for him and help him, and he was determined to be the very best dad he could be.

"I love you, too." He kissed Jake's head.

Now to deal with Victoria.

He found her still at the kitchen table, all the accordion pleats flattened and neatly stacked in rows. When she heard him she looked up.

Kyle pulled out the chair opposite her and sat down. "As upsetting as it is that Jake confided in me and not you, this one time, I think it's important to point out that he told one of us. He has two parents who love him and he needs to know he can come to either one of us."

"You're right," Victoria said, but her eyes didn't meet his. "It's just…the first time he wouldn't talk to me, wouldn't let me fix the problem. I feel so…helpless. I don't like it."

"Part of the reason he wanted to talk to me was to ask me to teach him how to fight."

Victoria jerked up. "Absolutely not. Animals fight," she snapped. "Uncivilized people fight. I will not have my son thinking it's okay to resolve a conflict with his fists." She didn't say it, but "like you were about to do Saturday night" hung in the air between them.

"I didn't say I would." Kyle sat back in his chair. "But what if I wanted to? Victoria, you need to understand you are not a single parent anymore.

You do not get to make all the decisions. I'm Jake's father and I have a say. Fifty-fifty."

She tried to say something but Kyle held up his hand to silence her.

"Let me finish. I know I wasn't here for the first eight years of Jake's life. But I'm here now. And I expect us to discuss things, to compromise and present a united front."

She rubbed the back of her neck. "I can do that. But I can't condone Jake fighting."

"I know that. And neither can I. I'm thinking more along the lines of signing him up for a martial arts class. I've taken a few over the years and the focus is on personal safety. He'll meet some new kids, gain confidence. I'll sit in on the classes so I can keep tabs on exactly what they're teaching him."

"How does Jake feel about it?"

"I haven't mentioned it, yet. I wanted to discuss it with you first."

"I appreciate that. Thank you. If he wants to take a karate class, would you see if you can find one on Wednesday nights when I have class?"

"I'll look into it tomorrow."

"Yay," Jake said, running into the kitchen. "My

friend Jimmy takes karate. He's not scared of nothing."

"Not scared of anything," Victoria corrected. "You snoop."

"I'm sorry, Mom," Jake said without any prompting. "I don't hate you. I love you every piece of sand on every beach in the whole wide world."

"Wow." Victoria opened her arms, her lips curving into the first smile he'd seen in days. Jake stepped into her embrace. "That's an awful lot." She kissed his head. "I love you, too, sweetie. A million, gajillion, patrillion red M&Ms."

"Yum," Jake said.

Victoria whispered something in Jake's ear. They each held out an arm to him. "Come on, Dad," Jake said. "Family hug."

Kyle wedged himself in, staking his place in their family unit, surrounding Victoria and Jake in his love. He kissed each one on the top of the head.

Victoria gazed up at him with heartfelt appreciation and mouthed the words, "Thank you." Then she set her cheek to his chest. He held her close, feeling the bond between them that nothing could break, feeling hope that a future together was still possible.

"I'm hungry," Jake said.

"I'll get dinner ready." She turned to Kyle. "Will you join us?"

There was no place he'd rather be. "If I can let Tori chill out downstairs."

"Sure."

Over dinner Jake retold his story to Victoria and the three of them hashed out a plan for what to do. The following morning Kyle accompanied his family to meet with the principal and the school social worker.

Afterwards Jake said, "My eye is sore. Can I take today off from school?"

Victoria glanced at her watch. "I've got a hospital-wide quality-assurance meeting in twenty minutes."

"I have a patient meeting I can't miss at eleven," Kyle said. "If Jake can hang with you in your office from eleven to twelve, I can take him now and stay with him for the afternoon," Kyle offered. "And if you could wrap your day up a little early, I'll work an evening shift tonight."

"You will? Are you sure?"

"Positive. Parents have been flexing their schedules for years. It won't be a problem." Victoria stepped close and said, "You were very impressive in there." She flicked her head toward the principal's office. "Very fatherly."

"Thank you."

She fingered the knot of his tie and added, "Have I told you how much I like your new look?"

"Actually, no. You haven't."

"Well, I do. A lot."

Which is exactly what he wanted.

For the rest of the week Kyle barely saw Victoria. At work she spent hours behind her closed office door working on some super-secret project. And at home, after dinner, she holed up in her home office, leaving Kyle to occupy Jake and get him ready for bed. Kyle loved every minute of it.

On Thursday night, while lying in Jake's bed listening to his son read from one of his favorite books, Kyle decided that no matter what the outcome of Friday's vote, whether he could continue to take Tori to work with him or not, he would accept the full-time position the hospital had offered him. He needed the job, needed to be close to his family, and, if he had to, he'd find a way to make his program effective without Tori's assistance.

After an unusually restless night, on Friday morning Kyle sat outside the administrative conference room with Tori, waiting to learn her fate, hoping he hadn't made a gross miscalculation by making his hire contingent on Tori's acceptance as an official hospital therapy dog. If the nursing director had her way, Tori *and* Kyle would be sent packing. And since he'd refused to sign on for anything more than a thirty-day temporary work detail, there wasn't anything he'd be able to do about it.

The door opened and Victoria, dressed in a high-powered tan business suit, stepped out.

Wow. "What's going on in there?" Kyle asked.

"They're about to vote."

"Then what are you doing out here?"

"I recused myself. I didn't want there to be any question of the validity of the results based on partiality."

That left three for and three against.

"I've done all I can." She walked toward him. "Bend down."

He did and she wrapped her arms around his neck and kissed him. Right there in the hallway for the administrative offices.

"Good luck," she said.

"No matter what happens, I'm not leaving town."

"I'm glad." Victoria smiled. "Jake likes having you here."

"And what about you?" Kyle asked. "Do you like having me here?"

"You're growing on me," she teased.

The door to the conference room opened and four people funneled out. The nursing director said, "You can come in now, Dr. Karlinsky. And you..." she pointed at Victoria accusingly "...meet me in my office at four o'clock."

"Can you pick up Jake?" Victoria asked with no show of emotion.

What the heck was going on? "Sure."

"Come, Dr. Karlinsky. Let's get this over with," the director said.

Her "Let's get this over with" did not sound promising. "I'll meet you at home," Victoria said.

Kyle liked the sound of that—*home*—and found himself grinning like a fool as he entered the conference room. Only Dr. Starzi and the nursing director remained.

"Have a seat." The director motioned to the chair on her left.

Dr. Starzi slid a thick report in a shiny blue cover across the table at him.

"What's this?" Kyle asked.

"A forty-two-page report, complete with bar graphs and colored pie charts, detailing the minutiae of all you and your dog have accomplished in the month you've been here," Dr. Starzi said. "Articles and dissertations highlighting the benefits of therapy dog programs in hospitals across the country. Testimonials from your patients and hospital staff. Mine is on page thirty-two, I believe." He leaned his elbows on the table. "You, my friend, have won the girlfriend lottery. Much to my chagrin."

Kyle picked up the report and flipped through it. "Victoria did all this?" For him?

"I hope you realize what you have," the director said. "By daring to go behind my back, by presenting this report without my prior knowledge and recusing herself from a vote I insisted she participate in, that girl put her future as director of nursing in jeopardy. For you."

Kyle didn't know what to say. He stood. Had to get to her, thank her, tell her how much he loved her, appreciated her. But first… "I don't want this position if Victoria has to pay for it by forfeiting her dream."

"True love. How sweet," Dr. Starzi said in true cynical form. "Tell him the outcome of the vote so I can get out of here." He checked his watch. "I have a sudden urge for a drink."

"Five for. One against," the director said. "Welcome on staff, Dr. Karlinsky. And you, too, Tori." She looked under the table where Tori lay curled at his feet. "The paperwork is waiting for you in Human Resources."

Kyle should have been thrilled. But… "You won't find anyone better to replace you," he said to the director. "Victoria is the best candidate you have and you know it. No one will do as good a job as she will."

"You let me worry about my replacement, Dr. Karlinsky. Good day." And with that she collected her papers and left the conference room.

Kyle checked every place in the hospital he thought Victoria might be. Every place but where she actually was. And by 3:45 p.m. he couldn't put off leaving any longer. He had to pick up Jake.

Victoria dropped her briefcase, slipped off her heels, and unbuttoned the top two buttons of her blouse. It was good to be home.

Kyle met her at the top of the stairs, a beer in one hand, a glass of white wine, which he held out to her, in the other. "You've had a busy week," he said.

Yes. She had. "Where's Jake?" Obviously not rushing to welcome his mother home with a hug and a kiss.

"At Ali's. I wasn't sure what shape you'd be in when you got home." He studied her like he could find the answer in her expression.

"What would you say…" she took the wine, walked past him to the couch in the living room and sat down "…if I told you I quit my job and as soon as I can sell my house I'm leaving town?" She took a sip of the Chardonnay.

Kyle sat down beside her, placed his beer on

a coaster on the coffee table and lifted her feet onto his lap. "I'd say let's try someplace warm where Jake can play baseball year round."

Good answer. He worked his thumbs into the arch of her right foot. "Man, that feels good." She closed her eyes, dropped her head against the back of the sofa and let him massage away the stress of the day.

"I saw the report you did," Kyle said. "Impressive stuff."

"Interesting subject matter."

"You shouldn't have put your promotion in jeopardy because of me," Kyle said.

She looked into his eyes. "It was the right thing to do. The hospital needs you and Tori."

"Is that the only reason you did it, because the hospital needs us?"

"It's the only reason I'll admit to." She smiled. "Do the other one." She slid her left foot into his talented grip. "I'm not an easy woman," she said. A gross understatement. But if he planned to stick around he needed to know the extent of it.

"Nothing worthwhile comes easy," Kyle replied.

"I'm a fiercely independent, high-strung perfectionist with a compulsive need to succeed. And when I get focused in on something it's hard to get me to stop."

Kyle moved his hand up her left shin. "That last one's not always a bad thing."

"And I still have…issues." That she hadn't managed to work all the way through. She took another sip of wine.

"You're also a deeply passionate and compassionate person." He caressed her knee and thigh. "An excellent mother, a loyal friend, and the woman I've fallen in love with."

Her eyes shot open.

"We all have issues, Victoria," he continued, as if he hadn't just professed his love for her. "As much as you strive to be, no one is perfect."

"Back up," Victoria said. "You've fallen in love with me?"

"To be honest," he said, "I think more correct phrasing would be I'm still in love with you. I'm not sure I ever stopped."

"Lord help you. Do you have any idea how high maintenance I am?"

He smiled confidently. "I can handle you."

She moved her feet to the floor and climbed onto his lap, straddling him. "You think so?"

"I know so."

"Good." She leaned in. Millimeters from his lips she said, "Because I love you, too." And she kissed him.

When they finally broke for air Kyle asked, "So are you going to tell me what happened in your meeting with the director?"

"It was all a test." Victoria unknotted Kyle's tie. "To see if I would blindly follow her or cave in to the pressure, or if I would stand up for what was in the best interest of the hospital."

Kyle stiffened beneath her. "Why, that conniving…"

"Shh." She put a finger to his lips. "She's the last thing I want to discuss right now." She slid his tie out from his collar and unbuttoned the two top buttons of his shirt.

"So you're still up to replace her?"

Victoria nodded and proceeded to work her way down the row of buttons keeping his beautiful chest from her view.

He grabbed her hands to stop her. "I need you to know I can be an asset at your fancy dinners.

I promise I will do my best to never embarrass you again."

"All I want, Kyle Karlinsky, is for you to be the wonderful man Jake and I love." She thought about it for a second. "Well, there's something else I want, too."

"Anything," Kyle said.

"Make love to me. Like you did that night in your car. I need to feel your weight on top of me, to know I can get through it."

His eyes met hers. "Are you sure?"

"I'm ready. I love you and I trust you."

Kyle lifted her off his lap. Her foot landed on a pack of Jake's baseball cards. Shoot. "When do we have to pick up Jake?"

Kyle took her hand and led her toward the bedroom. "I packed his overnight bag and told Ali if we weren't there by eight he'd be sleeping over."

"A planner," Victoria said. "How *did* I get so lucky?"

"That's nothing," Kyle said as he pulled her through the doorway toward her bed. "In about twenty minutes I'll show you the full extent of your luckiness."

She didn't need to wait. She already knew.

EPILOGUE

Three months later

"WHERE'S Kyle?" Roxie asked.

The employee of the month recognition dinner was due to start in five minutes, and Kyle, Mr. April, had yet to arrive. "Jake had his championship baseball game this afternoon." Victoria had stayed long enough to watch her son score the winning run and wave up to him when the coach walked by, carrying Jake on his shoulders. Then she'd run home to shower. "Afterwards, Kyle took him for pizza with the team while I came early to set up. He promised he'd be on time."

With another surprise. She'd begged him not to. She inhaled. Exhaled. It'd be fine. Whatever he wore would be fine, because she loved him and accepted him. And what could be worse than jeans?

"Who's Mr. Freakishly Tall, Pale, and Bald?" Roxie asked.

"Kyle's friend, Fig. He's in town for the week. Come, I'll introduce you."

"Fig," Victoria said to the polite, well-dressed man she'd met fifteen minutes earlier. "This is my friend Roxie, a recipient of your generosity in sponsoring our table."

"Nice to meet you." Fig held out his hand.

Roxie shook it. "Man, you're all bones. You feel like you could use a good meal."

"Right back atcha," Fig countered, without missing a beat.

"So take me to dinner," Roxie said. "Friday night. You choose the place."

Gotta love Roxie.

"I'm dying of cancer," Fig said without emotion.

Victoria tried to tell if he was joking, but his expression gave nothing away.

"Do you plan to do it before Friday night?" Roxie asked, because no one rattled Roxie.

Fig shrugged. "Not sure."

"Tell you what. I'll plan for you to pick me up at six. If you're not there by seven, I'll say a prayer."

Fig's smile showed a warm, playful side that matched Roxie's. "Deal," he said, holding out his hand again. Roxie shook it, again.

"Come on," Roxie said to Fig. "I'll give you my address."

"May I have your attention?" The MC's voice came through the speakers.

Kyle was late. Had something happened?

"If you all would turn your attention towards the lobby doors," the MC added.

Victoria turned. Her heart stopped, her breath caught in her lungs. There stood Kyle, gorgeous in a form-fitting tuxedo and shiny shoes. And he'd brought Jake, his mini red-haired replica in an identical tiny tux. Both carried one long-stemmed red rose. Jake also held a small white paper sack that looked to be from her favorite chocolate shop.

A hush fell over the room.

Kyle scanned the crowd until he found her. They locked eyes. He held out his hand, Jake took it, and together they started toward her. Father and son. Her two favorite men, the loves of her life, Kyle with a half-smile, Jake, shoulders back, chin up, proud to be part of something important.

When they got within five feet of her, Victoria quipped, "You can't keep from making a spec-tacle of yourself, can you?"

"Baby, you ain't seen nothing yet." Standing

an arm's length away, he reached into his pants pocket, took out a black velvet ring box, and went down on one knee.

His face very serious, Jake went down on one knee, beside him.

Victoria sucked in a breath. Her heart started to pound. Her eyes burned to let go of some tears.

Kyle looked up. So did Jake, full of hope.

Kyle held out the ring box and flipped open the lid to reveal a beautiful pear-shaped diamond set in an ultra-modern white-gold tension setting. Magnificent. A ring she would have chosen if given the opportunity.

"You have to say yes, Mom." Jake held up the white bag. "He even got you chocolates." A few laughs broke out in the silence.

"Say yes to what, Jake?" She raised her eyebrows and tilted her head, looking straight at Kyle. "No one's asked me anything."

She hoped she could hear him over the pulse pounding in her ears.

"Don't be difficult." Roxie elbowed her in the arm.

"Victoria Forley," Kyle said, "I don't deserve you, but I love you and Jake more than anything. And if you agree to marry me I promise to make you smile when you're sad, calm you when you're mad, and hold you in my arms until you're glad."

Jake tugged on Kyle's jacket. He leaned down and Jake whispered in his ear.

"You sure?" Kyle asked. Jake gave a solemn nod.

Kyle turned back to Victoria and added, "And I promise to give you a baby girl so you don't feel like it's two against one."

A few more laughs ensued.

Victoria smiled through the urge to cry, touched by their sincerity and Jake's concern.

"Well, in that case," she said, "how can I refuse? Yes. I'd be honored to marry you."

The crowd erupted in cheers.

"Thank you, Mommy. Thank you!" Jake said, jumping up and down.

Kyle slipped the ring onto her finger. A perfect fit. People tapped silverware against their glasses until she and Kyle kissed.

"Congratulations to the happy couple," the MC said. "Now, if you'll all take your seats, we can get started."

After the award ceremony the director came over to their table, rubbing her hands together.

"Young love makes people feel generous. Come on, you two. Let's mingle."

Not sure if Kyle would want to, Victoria turned to him. "Of course," he said with a congenial smile, placed his napkin on the table and stood.

Later, standing in the arms of the man she loved, her fiancé, swaying on the dance floor with dozens of other couples but feeling like she and Kyle were the only two people in the room, Victoria looked up and said, "Tonight was supposed to be *your* special night. In so much of a hurry you couldn't wait until tomorrow to propose?"

Kyle looked deeply into her eyes and replied, "You saying yes is what made tonight special. And long engagement, short engagement, big wedding, small wedding, courthouse wedding or Vegas wedding doesn't matter to me, as long as when it's over you're my wife."

She felt exactly the same way. "The sooner we're married, the sooner we can start working on that baby girl."

He lost the beat of the music, tightened his hold to keep her from tripping. "I've been thinking," he said. "Maybe we should hold off on that for a while, or I'm fine with us only having one child."

"You don't want another child?" While Jake's suggestion had taken her by surprise, the more she'd thought about it, the more she'd started to love the idea of having another baby, of having Kyle there with her this time.

"No. I mean I do. But…" He spun her to the edge of the dance floor where it was less crowded. "I think you should apply to medical school. I can help you study for the medical college admission tests. I'll support us and take care of Jake. It's been your dream since you were a little girl. Now there's nothing to stop you from going after it."

Victoria settled her ear against his chest, and while listening to the wild beat of his heart considered it—for less than thirty seconds. The long hours of study and residency that would have her working around the clock and keep her away from her husband and son. Years ago she'd wanted to become a physician to find cures for diseases, to help people. And she was helping people as a nurse. As director of nursing she'd have the ability to improve the quality of care provided to hundreds of patients at a time.

She looked up at the man willing to put their lives together on hold, to forgo having another child so she could pursue her childhood dreams, and fell even deeper in love with him.

But her dreams had changed. "Are you trying to renege on your promise to make a baby girl with me?"

"No, I…"

"Because I love you, Kyle Karlinsky. And if you think you can marry me then send me off to medical school, you've got another think coming."

"I thought…"

"You thought wrong. I'm happy with my life, sharing each day with you and Jake. And the only thing that would make me happier is a baby, girl or boy, within the next two years."

"I love you, too, Victoria, soon to be Karlinsky. And since I'm all about making you happy…" he pulled her close and nuzzled her ear the way she liked "…I promise to do everything within my power to meet that goal, or die from exhaustion, trying."

* * * * *